ABOUT THE AUTHOR

Andrew Langley started writing professionally over thirty years ago to accompany his work as a photojournalist. In a wide-ranging career that has seen him travel the world, his work has featured in national newspapers, a number of books and on television. Following the onset of multiple sclerosis, Andrew now lives a more sedentary lifestyle, creating his new adventures on paper. Andrew's other novels include *Mirror on the Soul* and *Dark Nights of the Soul*.

Praise for Andrew Langley's novels:

'Page-turning. I love these books.'
Louise Harnby, The Book Reviewers.

'An enjoyably scary romp.'
The BookLife Prize in Fiction.

'Gripping and original, with unforgettable characters.'
Jack Magnus for US review site, Readers' Favorite – 5-star review.

'Great ghost story.'
Invested Ivana for OneBookTwo Reviews.

'Atmospheric and entertaining thriller, told with style and humour.'
Karol Griffiths, Hollywood script editor.

I0592856

ALSO BY ANDREW LANGLEY:

Mirror on the Soul
Dark Nights of the Soul

SILENCE OF THE SOUL

Andrew Langley

Copyright © 2018 by Andrew Langley

All rights reserved. This book or any portion thereof may not be reproduced or used in any manner whatsoever without the express written permission of the author except for the use of brief quotations in a book review or scholarly journal.

Cover image copyright © 2018 by Andrew Langley

Typeset in Minion Pro

British Library Cataloguing in Publication Data. A catalogue record for this book is available from the British Library.

ISBN 978-0-9554137-9-7

Published by LPS Creative Media
www.lpscreativemedia.com

AUTHOR'S NOTE
This novel is a work of fiction. Names, characters, places and incidents are either the product of the author's imagination or are used fictionally. Any resemblance to actual events, locales or persons, living or dead, is entirely coincidental.

To discover more about the Nathen Turner novels, and read news, views and extracts, visit: www.andrewlangley.co.uk

DEDICATION

For my brothers, lifelong friends.

CHAPTER 1 – A CRY FOR HELP

The brackish tang of the sea wafted in through the kitchen window and enveloped the two figures huddled across the table. There was a tension between them, like two strangers meeting for the first time and forcing a conversation. The taller figure sighed, sank into his chair and said, 'Okay, Molly, let's go again from the beginning.'

Molly pulled herself upright, tried to regain her composure, failed, and pounded the table with her fist, spilling tea from her cup in the process. 'It's like I told you, Nathen. After my dad died, this slick piece of crap turned up on the doorstep and started saying he had messages from my father. You know, from beyond the grave.' She jerked her head towards her seated companion with the look of a boxer staring down her next opponent.

Nathen Turner eased his lanky frame out of the chair and moved to switch on the kettle as she squinted up at him, tapping her painted fingernails on the table.

Molly Craggs had a face that lived up to her name. Pointed chin, thin nose and close-set blue eyes surrounded by a cropped mess of gelled brown spiky hair. Her narrow gaze lasered through Turner as he poured the hot water into two plain mugs, pulled out the sopping teabags and flopped them into the bin. Turner had spent the bulk of his adult life reading people for a living. It didn't take a rocket scientist to figure out that this was a lady you crossed at your peril, and he'd need to tread carefully. He deliberately slowed down his actions in an attempt to calm the mood. He smoothed his blue Hawaiian shirt, placed the mugs on the table, removed the spilt drink, and sat back down, hoping the distraction of the fresh tea would pacify his angry guest.

Turner blew across the top of his steaming brew. 'So what were these messages exactly?' He cocked his head, leaning in as if the whole subject fascinated him. It didn't, and he still had no idea what this fearsome female wanted from him. All he'd picked up so far was that a clairvoyant had called in to see Molly's recently widowed mother and offered his help to bring comfort and closure to her grief. What Molly's problem was with that, he still struggled to grasp. And why she'd turned up on *his* doorstep to vent her frustration remained a complete mystery. He'd never met this seething bundle of resentment before and he was silently praying he'd never have that privilege again.

Molly yanked a crumpled piece of paper from her handbag and perched a pair of horn-rimmed reading glasses on her nose. Now, she looked even more angular as she thrust her face closer to read her writing. 'He turned up at my mother's retirement property on the edge of town and starting asking stupid questions. Here ... I wrote some of them down so I'd remember them. Look at this one ... "Where did a bell ring that nobody could explain?"' She took a mouthful of her tea and closed her eyes briefly before continuing.

Turner's laid-back mood was rubbing off on her, but not enough for him to stop worrying about her mental stability. On the inside, he was far from composed, but his life working in the spiritual community, encountering many weird and wonderful characters, had made him an expert at hiding his real feelings.

Molly curled back the bottom of the paper so she could read more. 'So my mother says she has no idea, so he changes it to ... hang on ...' Peeling back more of the tatty page, she said, '... he changes it to, "Do you understand about a telephone ringing and you going to pick it up, thinking no one was there?" So guess what she told him? I mean, honestly.'

Back in familiar territory, Turner said, 'She told him the phone had rung after her husband had died and that there was no one on the end of it, right?' He pulled the paper from her hand and scanned the rest of the scribbled notes.

Molly nodded vigorously at Turner, her contempt for what had happened to her mother written clearly across her face. 'Correct!' she said, raising her arms as if swatting away invisible flies. 'And then he tells her that the telephone ringing is a message from heaven, and my dad's way of letting her know he's at peace now. I mean, what the hell is all that about? Do you know how many calls you get when someone dies? The bank, the phone company, utilities – all usually from some crappy call centre or another with a dodgy line connection. I mean, come on. He's a con man, Nathen, I'm telling you.'

Turner tapped his feet noiselessly under the table, unsure where this was leading. Thinking back to his past, when he'd been a fake psychic medium and hadn't believed in any spiritual realm, he recalled pulling similar stunts himself to turn a dishonest buck. Fake, that is, until he'd unwittingly opened a portal into the spirit world and the ghost of a young girl had come calling at his door. He now knew there was a world beyond our knowledge – something spiritual, something supernatural – and he spent his days studying old texts, trying to find out more. After quitting his fake act, he'd been contacted by many lost souls from the afterlife looking for his help. The experiences had left him with an affinity with the spirit world that he'd never truly understood, but he'd developed a sort of psychic sixth sense, as if he'd tuned into some supernatural radio channel that he couldn't switch off. Now Turner was as far removed from this alleged con man as a butterfly from a shark. The phone ploy after the death of a loved one had been standard fare in his old profession. But, if he admitted as much, would he be tarring himself with the same brush in Molly's eyes?

Struggling to understand what this had to do with him, and why this formidable lady had come knocking on his door, Turner slurped at his tea, absentmindedly backing up from the intimidating force of nature that sat glaring at him from across the table. Thinking it best he find out the whole story and let his visitor rant herself into a calmer frame of mind, he said, 'I still don't understand how he met your mother in the first place. You say he just turned up out of the blue?'

Molly snorted. 'Exactly – he just appeared on the

doorstep, saying he was a clairvoyant and that he'd received an important spirit message from my father.'

To Turner it was obvious that this alleged clairvoyant had been scanning the Deaths, Births and Marriages section in the local newspaper for names and picked out a likely target. In this modern age of the Internet, it would have been fairly straightforward for him to trace an address, check out any Facebook and other social media entries, news stories and the like, and build a picture of the deceased husband's life without ever having known him. By throwing in the odd fact or two from this research, the man would have easily presented the information as a demonstration of his clairvoyant ability. He'd done exactly the same thing himself in his shamming days, but he had no intention of telling Molly Craggs that.

Instead, still hoping she'd get to the end of her tale and explain what she wanted, he said, 'Tell me more about this guy – his name, appearance, anything you've got.' Perhaps feigning an interest would speed things up and get his unwanted guest to leave as soon as possible. He didn't have it in his heart to simply turn her away. She was clearly suffering, and he felt, no, knew that Molly believed Turner could lift her burden somehow.

Another crumpled piece of paper was dutifully peeled from its hiding place in the grubby brown handbag and passed across the table. It was a two-sided flyer with a list of show dates and a brief biography of a man called Hugh Williams. Turner smoothed out the wrinkled page and then sat and read it silently to himself.

Hugh Williams – The People's Clairvoyant

International personality and TV star Hugh Williams is the best-loved clairvoyant in the UK. Known by many for his successful radio and TV appearances around the world, Hugh has the incredible ability of second sight and uses it to channel messages from the spirit world to our earthly realm. He first felt his calling as a child when he brought comfort to a close friend who'd recently lost her parents. Now, due to popular demand, Hugh demonstrates his phenomenal abilities in a range of shows around the country. Prepare to be amazed ...

And so it went on, followed by the obligatory 'For entertainment purposes only' rider in tiny print at the bottom of the page. Turner had to laugh. If you were going to tell a lie, make it a big and preposterous one – in Turner's experience these were less likely to be questioned. He'd been in the industry for around two decades now and he'd never heard of 'best-loved' Hugh Williams. The TV and radio claim likely meant Williams had appeared on some obscure satellite or cable channel. This style of con was an old one, much used by the medicine men of the Wild West and their infamous elixirs that could cure every ailment on the planet. Shout it loud and confidently enough and the fiction would be taken as fact. He idly wondered how many politicians still relied on this in their day job, making claim and counterclaim to each other and a gullible nation. Realising he was getting off track, he turned his attention back to Molly.

After scanning the flyer for any images, Turner found only endorsements of the clairvoyant's show from names that were possibly made up. Maybe he did know this guy from when he used to do his psychic shows, but Turner still didn't recognise the stage name. Searching for other clues to the man's identity, he said, 'So, what does he look like?'

Sucking in her cheeks, Molly said, 'Got a face like a weasel chewing on a lemon. I think that's why they haven't put his photo on – they don't want to scare the children.'

Turner cracked up. Blowing her cheeks back out in a chuckle, Molly smiled, unclenched her fists, leaving red marks where her fingernails had dug into her palms, and drained the last of her tea. Sunlight streamed in through the kitchen window, sparkled across a pile of glasses stacked high in the sink and bathed the room in an array of darting reflections, adding a pleasing glow as the mood lifted between the pair.

Braving her wrath, Turner thought that now would be the best time to ask her how she believed he fitted in to this sorry tale. 'I'm still not sure what you want me to do. Sounds like you need the police, not the help of someone who coaches psychics. How is it you think I can help?'

These days, Turner ran a small but successful one-man band that taught palm reading, tarot cards and astrology to a willing group of loyal locals. Those who believed they had a psychic gift beat a steady path to his door as his reputation as a teacher had grown. He wasn't quite at the guru stage yet, but word of mouth had built his small enterprise into a successful business. Only last week, an American tourist had spent a pleasant afternoon learning the basics of astrology.

Turner loved these one-on-one sessions; sharing his interest in all things supernatural with a diverse group of people always proved interesting, each bringing their own fascinating metaphysical stories. Molly's story was an alien intrusion into his cosy world of believers, and he wriggled uncomfortably on his chair, waiting for her answer.

Molly leant forward, pushed her empty mug to one side and locked eye contact to make sure she had his full attention. 'The guys at The Alchemist said you were the man for the job if I needed someone to check whether a clairvoyant had a spiritual gift and wasn't making it all up.'

The Alchemist was a small, purple-fronted spiritual shop five minutes' walk away from Turner's home in Whitby. It was also the home of two of his oldest friends. He mentally reminded himself to thank them in person by throttling them the next time they met.

Turner squirmed as if his seat were made of sandpaper. Exposing someone publicly was not his style – whoever this man was, he'd rather leave him alone. He'd been in this guy's shoes, and would rather give him the benefit of the doubt. Perhaps the clairvoyant's motives were pure, but his methods lacked the finesse to pass as the genuine article. Maybe the clairvoyant had just started out, or truly believed he had a gift to help people connect with their departed relatives. Turner had seen this many times with spiritual workers. The longer they'd worked in the profession, the stronger their belief in their own powers, as more and more punters swooned at their ability to perceive things they couldn't possibly know. But the truth was much simpler – the more clients they worked with, the better their intuition became.

Sitting across from a typical middle-aged female client, it became easy to spot if they were struggling with marital breakdowns or career pressures.

He knew; he'd been there. Most of Turner's ex-clientele were products of society's expectations and had lost their true identity in a bid to conform. Gone were their dreams of childhood in a drive to fit in with their peer group. When Turner, in his fake psychic guise, had pointed out to them that they had untapped potential and that they felt something held them back, delivered as if he'd received the information from the spirit realm, his unsuspecting clients had gasped in wonder.

Such was Turner's past, and he didn't want to go anywhere remotely near it. He hoped Molly Craggs would put the whole thing down to experience and move on.

Trying to find a way out, he said, 'Well that's all very flattering, but that is not what I do.'

Bank notes flew wildly across the table, skidding to a halt next to Turner's elbow. 'Here's a hundred pounds. That will cover tickets and expenses,' Molly said, pushing the money closer to the psychic's hands.

Turner backed away from the cash as if it carried some fatal disease. 'Tickets? Tickets for what?'

Molly picked up the flyer and pointed. 'He's on at the Dancing Dog pub tonight. It's only twenty minutes away – down the Bridlington Road. I just want you to see the show and tell me if he's a fraud. Then I can tell my mother, and put an end to this whole thing. Look, he's taken my mum for around two thousand pounds already; this is an investment. Take it. Please, I'm begging you.' Her eyebrows fluttered like two spiny birds trying to land on a cliff.

A beautiful Japanese face peered from the top of the stairs leading down into the kitchen. Ebony hair hung down to the shoulder, draping a smooth olive face twinkling with a pair of stunning green eyes.

Green Eyes stepped cautiously into the kitchen, taking in the strange woman leaning towards Turner as if she'd passed him a cache of drug money. 'Everything okay?' Green Eyes said, moving closer. 'I thought I heard a fight down here a while ago.'

Turner smiled to himself, glad of the distraction. He watched dainty bare feet, under a pair of black skinny jeans, padding lightly across the floor like a panther hunting for prey. He waved an 'everything's fine' gesture but to the green-eyed panther it looked like a shrug so she inched closer, tensing slightly. Turner could see the concern on her face, and the words tumbled from his mouth. 'No ... no, everything's fine. Molly, this is Jade, my wife. Jade, meet Molly Craggs.'

Backing off, Jade allowed her body to relax. She forced an embarrassed smile, stretched out a soft hand and then nodded hello. Jade worked as an airline stewardess and could turn on the charm like a switch. Dealing with drunk and abusive passengers had taught her to mask her true emotions well, but she remained suspicious of the their unexpected visitor's motives.

Turner read the question on Jade's face as she scanned the bank notes on the table and said, 'Molly wants me to tell her if some clairvoyant guy I've never heard of is a fraud.'

Unsure whether Turner was joking, Jade raised her

eyebrows and looked curiously at her husband. This seemed way too serious for a prank, so she simply said, 'Oh, I see.' But she didn't see at all. Self-consciously pulling her thin silk blouse across her chest, she spotted the crumpled flyer on the table surrounded by a fistful of ten-pound notes. She picked it up and read it.

'This him?'

Turner nodded.

'Why, what's he done?'

Turner ignored the question, thinking it best not to get Molly started on her story again. All he needed now was her to launch herself into another rant after he'd tried so hard to calm her state of mind.

'Fancy taking in a clairvoyant show? It's on at the Dancing Dog tonight – might even be fun. All expenses paid.' Waving the cash, Turner smiled as if he'd offered his wife a once-in-a-lifetime opportunity.

Jade stood and took a mocking bow. 'Well I *am* flattered. You high rollers always take us chicks to the finest places.' The American twang in her voice was unmistakeable and she smiled back coyly, as if embarrassed about receiving a prestigious award.

Although of Japanese origin, she'd spent her childhood in the States and was no stranger to some over-the-top acting at her husband's expense. Jade knew the Dancing Dog pub and it was hardly the height of sophistication. Think working man's club meets a karaoke bar and you pretty much had it nailed. Stalking off, she glanced back at him with a gleam in her eye from the foot of the stairs. 'But if tonight turns out to be a pint-and-a-fight experience, you're a dead man.'

Turner looked across to the grinning face of Molly Craggs, who was thoroughly enjoying Jade's mini performance. Relaxing back in his chair and shrugging, he said, 'Well, Molly, I guess that means we're going.'

CHAPTER 2 – THE WEASEL IN SHADES

As he scanned the eccentric jumble of heaving humanity in the Dancing Dog, Turner hoped he was wrong about the clairvoyant he'd been asked to investigate. He'd prefer to discover a kindred spirit – someone also touched by the spirit realm; then he could report back to Molly that she had nothing to worry about.

Sipping on his shandy, he watched the multi-coloured clientele chatting gaily over their drinks, excited about the evening ahead. It certainly was a bizarre mix, like a hippy convention had been asked to join a golf-club dinner. But these were all *his* people, the same assorted masses that had attended *his* psychic shows, and he felt at home in their company. The feeling that gnawed deep inside him, though, was one of betrayal, as if he were acting as a kind of confidential informant in a police investigation against a friend. Deciding finally that he couldn't go through with it, he was about to leave and make his excuses to Jade by feigning an illness when someone nudged his arm.

'Sorry, I didn't mean to bump into you. I'm so excited about the show. Have you been to one of these before?' an attractive blonde in a low-cut dress said, interrupting his thoughts. She smiled at him and waved her ample bosom temptingly as she cut in front of Jade at his side.

'Yes, but I've never seen Hugh Williams before,' Turner said, embarrassed as he had inadvertently glanced down at her revealing dress before making eye contact.

Jade coughed in the background and covered a giggle as her husband's cheeks began to redden.

The blonde mirrored Turner's posture and brought her breathing rhythm in sync with his. 'Are you hoping to make contact with anyone in particular tonight?' she asked with an innocent smile.

Turner's heart sank. Having seen, and used, this method of information-gathering before a psychic show, he wondered what to do. If he was right, this woman was part of the crew acquiring intelligence from the crowd for the clairvoyant to use tonight.

Desperately hoping he was wrong about his new blonde acquaintance, and that she was just making small talk, he said, 'I'm hoping Hugh Williams can contact my wife. I've heard he's an excellent clairvoyant.' He raised a hand to wipe away a non-existent tear. 'My wife drowned six months ago. Left me with two little ones. It's so hard to raise young children on your own.'

All Williams had to do to contact Turner's wife was to come up and talk to her – she stood right next to him – but the blonde didn't know that. If she *was* part of the crew, then she'd feed the bogus story to the clairvoyant and he'd use it. If he didn't, even better, and Turner's suspicions would be put to rest.

To reinforce his story, Turner put on the saddest face

he could muster. 'It was a boating accident. Painful for me to talk about. I'm sorry ... my poor Rebecca.' He pulled out a white handkerchief to mop away more invisible tears and looked at the floor, gazing sadly at his snakeskin cowboy boots with the burnt toes.

The blonde's expression took on a mask of sorrow as she tenderly squeezed his forearm. 'I didn't mean to upset you. Perhaps I'd better let you pull yourself together rather than remind you of the pain. I'm sorry for your loss. You have my deepest sympathy.' And with that she whisked herself off into the crowd, smiling apologetically back at him.

'You think she's in on it, don't you?' Jade whispered as she watched the blonde disappear, leaning in so close he could feel her breath on his ear.

Turner nodded back at her. 'I hope I'm wrong, but did you see the way she matched the tone of my voice and my body language? That girl's an expert at rapport-building – I think she's part of the crew. If I'm right about her, our Mr Hugh Williams will be able to make miraculous contact with my fictitious and very-dead wife during his show. If I'm wrong, then great. We can all go home happy.'

Jade poked him hard in the ribs, causing him to spill his drink on the wooden floor. 'The way you were looking at her ... erm ... assets, you seem a bit too happy already!'

Turner laughed and kissed her on the forehead. 'Okay, I surrender – I'm only human. I *do* think that blonde's a ringer, though. To everybody else she's just another punter sharing some small talk before the show starts. But I think she's trotting from group to group to get titbits of inside information from the crowd. It's classic hot reading – it could be she's getting a few facts for our clairvoyant buddy to miraculously reveal, as if he's channelling messages from the spirits. It's much better than him taking educated guesses.'

'What do you mean, educated guesses?' Jade hadn't been around for most of Turner's fake psychic career. She had no real interest in that side of him and certainly wasn't privy to the inner workings of his methods.

Turner tried to explain, keeping his voice low so he couldn't be overheard. 'Say we've never met before and you come to me for a psychic reading. I pull out a deck of tarot cards, and then I tell you they have a secret power to reveal hidden things. I pretend to read the cards and say, "Between the ages of thirteen and seventeen there were many changes in your life", or something like that.'

Jade nodded and whispered, 'You know that's true. I moved to America with my father.'

'Exactly – but everybody experiences changes during those teenage years. The statement applies no matter what culture or background you're from.'

Jade nodded and moved closer to listen.

'The trick is to get someone to tell you about some of those experiences and then play them back in a way that makes it look like you're getting the information from the spirit world. So, if you tell me you moved abroad, I say something like "The cards tell me there was a lot of travel during that period, and you struggled to make new friends." Again, everybody experiences this when they move to a new area. The more information you give me, the more specific I can make the reading. Educated guesses – do you see?'

Jade did, and felt in awe of her husband's ability to

manipulate snippets of information in a way that made him look like some sort of supernatural spokesperson. The man she loved didn't need any gimmicks to contact the dead. Quite the opposite – they came looking for him whether he wanted it or not. Relieved he'd put this fraudulent side of his life behind him, Jade followed him over to the bar counter.

Turner picked up a postcard in a purple envelope with the title 'Messages to a friend' in bold black type. 'See these – they ask you to write a message of love or friendship to someone in the spirit world, seal it in the envelope and then put it in the basket over there for Hugh Williams to use during the show.'

Jade picked up the card and shrugged. 'But so what? That's a good thing if he can somehow pass those messages on, don't you think?'

Turner ran his finger under the questions. 'So why do they ask for your name, where you're sitting and the relationship you had with the person you're sending the message to? It even asks for your favourite memory of that person. With this much information it's not difficult to pretend to contact them in the spirit world – you have everything here. It even asks you to put in a photograph of them if you have one. Then the clairvoyant even knows what they look like.'

Jade thought for a moment. 'But when I've seen this type of thing before, the clairvoyant never opens the message until after they've given the reading. How can they know what's inside a sealed envelope?'

Turner put the card and envelope down, then moved away from the crowd and lowered his voice. 'You ever notice how nobody gets the envelopes back? They get the card and photo, but not the envelope.'

Again, Jade shrugged.

Not sure if he should tell his beautiful companion how the scam worked, Turner hesitated. Unwittingly, he'd blurted out details from the workings of his past life – a life he was trying hard to leave far behind. Tugging to straighten out his already straight shirt, he paused to clear invisible phlegm from his throat. He'd come too far to stop now.

After casting a few furtive glances around to make sure no one was in earshot, he said, 'They take away all the cards five or ten minutes before the show – you know that, right?'

Feeling as though she were listening to a magician reluctantly explaining a trick, Jade nodded.

'Okay, well once they're out of sight backstage, they open about a dozen of the messages, write the information on the outside of the envelope and seal it back up again. All the clairvoyant has to do is read what's written on the outside of the envelope and then destroy it afterwards so there's no incriminating evidence.'

Jade gasped and turned to watch the unsuspecting punters filling in the cards with hope in their hearts. With this small mystery shattered, she scanned the room for the blonde who'd approached them, and watched her through a different set of eyes. Turner was right – she chatted to different groups, and then moved on. Pushing her bosom out at the men and beaming a friendly smile at the women. It was like watching a masterclass in relationship-building, her smart green dress not too showy, and no ridiculous jewellery or tattoos to make her stand out. She was endearing and instantly forgettable at the same time.

The same could not be said about the rest of the gathering crowd. In the corner, a long-haired guy with a ponytail and a pierced nose talked excitedly to a small goth girl with huge Dr Marten boots, the mirror-polished toes gleaming in the room lights. Opposite, four well-to-do women were staring at the couple, making what looked like derogatory remarks about the state of the nation's youth. Bohemian arty types dressed in purples, yellows and blues discussed star signs and the importance of angels in the modern world. It was an eclectic mix and a testament to how the lure of spirituality seemed to cross all racial and class boundaries.

'Ladies and gentlemen,' a fat guy in a greasy polo shirt announced from the small stage. 'May I have your attention?'

No response; everyone ignored him. Obviously used to this kind of welcome, he waddled over to a PA speaker and waved the microphone in front of it. The ensuing feedback screech did the job.

'Thank you. The show will be starting in five minutes so if you'd be good enough to take your seats.' He waved his pudgy arms to indicate the rows of plastic chairs arranged in front of him. Job done, he disappeared backstage, accompanied by the scraping and metallic banging of chairs being pushed around and rearranged by the compliant throng.

The room itself was a purpose-built extension that the Dancing Dog had added about ten years previously to try to attract different clientele when the pub business had dwindled following the smoking ban. Burgundy wallpaper clung on for grim death, peeling and tearing at every angled opportunity. Paintings of cheap hunting scenes had been replaced by framed photos of past celebrity visitors, lopsidedly covering the worst of the damage; it looked like a cross between a teenager's bedroom and a madam's boudoir.

In the cellar, a bespoke microbrewery was bubbling away with this month's designer beers, whose advertising kept to the canine feel of the pub's name. Turner had tried the Wag lager and Pawfection real ale craft beers before, and had to admit they were pretty good. Yeasty beer fumes cocooned the room in a scent of hay fields and marmite, and drifted across the small stage to be absorbed by the heavy black curtains.

The PA rattled with a melodic out-of-key dirge pierced by a recorded American voice.

'Throughout human history,' it said in a deep, serious New York accent, 'man has been fascinated by the thought of an afterlife. The world inhabited by the dead – that hidden realm of spirits with their all-seeing power. Journey with us tonight as we step behind the veil and into the unknown. The show you're about to see doesn't involve tricks or gimmicks of any kind. What you're about to see is real. Now, please put your hands together and welcome the UK's best-loved clairvoyant, Hugh Williams.'

The smattering of clapping was cut short as the room was plunged into complete darkness, causing ripples of excitement to wash over the crowd. A bright centre flood beamed across the stage, blinding those in the front row after the temporary darkness. Williams brushed through the curtains at a run, accompanied by a loud fanfare of music.

'Thank you very much, ladies and gentlemen.' Williams had disguised his weasel features with a pair of green-tinted glasses, making him look like the clairvoyant love child of a rat and John Lennon. 'I invite you now to join me as we take a journey into the spirit world.'

The clairvoyant stepped down from the stage in his smart suit and walked through the audience, smiling constantly, keeping his hands clasped across his stomach. Non-threatening nice guy was the impression he tried to convey, and it was difficult not to warm to him and his pleasant bearing.

After heading back to the centre of the room, Williams paused to make sure he had everyone's attention. 'I don't claim to be a doctor or a psychiatrist, but I am a genuine clairvoyant. Any doubts you have I'm sure will drift away during our demonstration this evening. All my life I've been able to see visions of the future and connect with the hidden realm of the afterlife. Why or how this is, I truly cannot explain. I don't like to communicate bad news, but I must pass on everything I get from the spirit world. Perhaps the best thing is for me to show you.'

Turner had to hand it to the guy. Two minutes in and he already had the audience on the edge of their seats. Crossing his fingers unconsciously, Turner hoped again that he was wrong, and that this obviously accomplished showman was the real deal.

Smiling, Williams waved his hands vaguely over half of the audience on the other side of the room to Turner. 'Why do I need to go over here and talk about a window that was broken, but not by accident?'

Amid the seated watchers, one man leant forward and smiled at the remark. Williams spotted him.

'I'm settling on you, sir. Would you stand up, please?' Williams pointed directly at the man, who self-consciously struggled to his feet. Before he was fully upright, a brunette in a tight black Lycra ensemble emerged from the shadows and pushed a microphone into his hand.

'Sir, can you understand about a window being deliberately broken? Does that make sense to you?'

The nervous participant nodded.

'Into the microphone, if you would, please.'

The man confirmed it for all to hear, causing astonishment amongst the bohemian women sitting alongside.

'Sir, what I see is an older gentleman standing behind you. He's smiling at you and nodding his head.'

The bohemians squinted in the dark, looking for a shadowy figure behind the man.

'He's just saying to me, "Tell him I know now." He's telling me that everyone referred to him as the patriarch of the family – they called him something like "father" or "papa". Again, does that make sense to you, sir?'

'It's my father,' the man said simply, causing gasps among the bohemians, who were still scanning the darkened room looking for the ghostly figure.

Leaning forward to catch every syllable, the women were now completely engrossed in this incredible demonstration of spirit communication.

'Your father wants me to tell you, from the other side of life, that he's extremely grateful to you for what you've done for your mother.' Williams gazed kindly at the man, who started to tremble. 'The pain of the past three years will pass and you will feel you can move on now.'

Moving closer, Williams crowded the man's personal space and looked like a preacher about to convey a sacred blessing. 'Going back to the stone incident – the breaking of the window – you thought you'd got away with it, didn't you, and that no one would ever find out.'

The man smiled to himself as if remembering some mischief from his past. 'Yes, I did.'

'Well, I'm sorry, sir, but your father tells me he won't let you hide these things anymore.'

Laughter washed across the room.

The forefingers on both of Williams's hands touched his thumbs, creating a meditation-like pose. 'I'm happy to have made contact for you and leave his love with you.'

Loud ripples of applause accompanied the man as he sat down, and the Lycra brunette darted in to recover the microphone.

Turner could only admire Williams's approach and the way he appeared to be presenting specific information. But so far, the signs were not good. Most of the clairvoyant's spiel was classic cold reading – the ability to give a spiritual message with no prior information on the client.

Having worked the circuit as a fake psychic, Turner knew that most adult men had been involved in an incident where they'd broken a window and tried to cover it up. When the guy had leant forward smiling, it was obvious it had happened to him. Throwing in the non-specific patriarch figure standing behind him was sheer genius as it had allowed Williams to pretend it was a father, grandfather, uncle, brother or any strong male figure in the man's past. No one seemed to notice that he'd never asked the man to confirm the statements about the mother and the pain of the past three years. Maybe these parts had been provided courtesy of the pre-show blonde or maybe they'd been pure guesses.

This guy was good – Turner was enjoying the show, and he tried to keep an open mind about the clairvoyant's spiritual ability.

Williams placed his well-manicured hand over his neck as he walked back across the room towards Turner's side. 'Why am I seeing a letter "B"? And I have a choking feeling here – it's as if I can't breathe. A sound like "brick" or "beck" ... no wait a minute ... "Beccy".' Williams eased close enough for Turner to make out the pale lines on his pinstripe suit. 'Does the name Beccy or Rebecca mean anything to someone over here? I'm being drawn to this corner.' Williams zigzagged his way through the chairs. 'This is someone close to you, the love of your life.'

All hope that he'd found a kindred spirit drained from Turner. His guess about the pre-show blonde had been correct, and now he knew beyond any doubt that the clairvoyant was faking it.

Turner stood up and the microphone miraculously appeared in his hand, delivered by the Lycra ninja. He put on his best impression of an amazed widower and whispered, 'Yes, she was my wife.'

Jade stared at the floor, not trusting herself to look up, as gasps broke out in the crowd.

'Sir, she says it wasn't necessary for her to pass when she

did. There was some form of accident ... around here.' Williams rubbed his palm around the base of his throat. 'Does that make sense to you, sir?'

Turner pretended to cry and muttered between fake sobs, 'Yes.' But inside he felt devastated by having uncovered the scam, and his posture slumped as the clairvoyant stepped closer.

Reading this as a sign of grief, Williams said, 'Why am I getting a feeling like I can't breathe? And water, a sense of being surrounded by water. Sir, did your wife drown?' Williams would have already been told she had by the pre-show blonde, but he needed to play this out for effect.

'Yes, she did.'

Two women next to Turner muttered, 'Poor dear', and looked up at him with wet eyes.

Consoling now, Williams kept his voice low and reassuring. 'She wants me to tell you that it's time to move on with your life. It wasn't necessary for her to pass when she did, but that's sometimes just the way things are.'

Slowly, he edged forward so he could stand next to Turner, who was still doing his best sobbing impression.

'She says she loves you and is at peace now. You must move on with your life and look after your two children.'

Turner looked up at the clairvoyant's face, highlighted by the stage lighting, feigning surprise that Williams knew he had two, albeit imaginary, children. Now, up close, Turner saw the faint crescent scar on Williams's cheek ending in a mess of jagged lines. It was a unique shape that Turner recognised from his past, but the man this scar belonged to was not called Hugh Williams.

Squinting against the glare, Turner looked again. Yes, it was definitely the exact scar that he'd seen before; there could be no mistake. The facial features behind the tinted glasses were now taking on a familiar shape, stirring Turner's distant memories.

Both men recognised each other at the same time and Williams stopped dead in his tracks. Turner smiled and reached out his hand as he whispered away from the microphone, 'Hello, Paul. Fancy meeting you here. Or should I call you Hugh Williams now?'

Hidden from the audience, Williams's face drained of colour and took on an expression between shock and fear. Quickly recovering, he fixed a false smile on his face and whispered back, 'Not now, Nathen. Meet me backstage after the show … *please.*' The last word was drawn out, his eyes pleading. To the audience it simply looked as if the men were exchanging pleasantries off-microphone.

Turner gave the slightest of nods so no one else would notice. He watched as Williams moved away without a backward glance, launching his next spirit message to the other side of the room. What a pro, Turner thought, and sat back down.

CHAPTER 3 – VISIONS OF THE NILE

Without missing a beat, Williams eased around the room, calling on more and more invisible spirits – mothers, daughters, a myriad of assorted relatives – before closing the first half of the show using the 'Messages to a friend' envelopes and leaving to a huge round of applause.

Turner smiled at Jade as the clapping died down. 'Mystery solved. I know this guy. We've just received a personal invitation backstage after the show. Shouldn't be a problem to sort this out now, trust me.' He moved his hand over his heart as he spoke, feeling nothing but relief. This whole experience was one he'd rather get through as quickly as possible and move on with his life. He felt sure he'd be able to sort out Molly's concerns, and warn Williams off, with little trouble on either side.

Jade had questions but knew better than to interrogate her husband in such a public arena, so she simply said, 'Okay,' and headed to the bar for more drinks.

The crowd were now chatting eagerly about the performance so far, swapping stories of other clairvoyant events they'd been to, comforting each other in their common belief in the spiritual realm. Those who'd been singled out were the most animated, their faces filled with relief.

Turner knew the whole show tonight was a sham, but felt he had no right to disturb their moment of peace, so he stayed silent and observant. He was beginning to enjoy himself, despite his misgivings. The whole spiritual realm fascinated and excited him, and he loved being around open-minded people who shared its allure. Listening in on as many conversations as he could without appearing like an eavesdropper, he was just picking up on a dramatic story about a tarot-card reading when Jade returned, juggling the drinks as she moved through the crowd.

As she squeezed herself back onto the seat, Turner caught a satisfying glimpse of her shapely behind in tight jeans, and silently reminded himself how lucky he was to be married to this beautiful woman.

The PA system shattered his lustful thoughts as the fat guy in the greasy polo shirt returned. 'Ladies and gentlemen,' he said, trying to sound as commanding as possible. They were ignoring him again. This time he tapped on the mic, sending a series of sharp pops, like gunshots, around the room. Turner wondered whether the guy had earned his stripes in the bear pits of the working-men's clubs. He certainly had a knack for getting people's attention.

'Ladies and gentlemen,' Polo Shirt said again. Now all eyes turned to the stage and he allowed himself a brief smirk of satisfaction.

Turner had been right. Polo-shirt man had spent over a decade corralling audiences in a series of dingy clubs where keeping the audience down to three fights a night was a major success. The colourful crowd in the Dancing Dog that evening was a push-over in his eyes.

'We have a very special guest for the second part of the show. She really is the eighth wonder of the world.'

'Bloody hell, they've got Dolly Parton,' Turner quipped, now in better humour, and got a sharp dig in the ribs for his trouble from Jade, followed by angry shushes from behind.

'Ladies and gentlemen, please welcome Princess Amunet.' He pronounced it 'ah-moon-et', and waddled off the stage into the blackness of the wings.

A feeling of unease crept over Turner as if a freezing night fog had oozed into his pores. Icy chills rattled his skinny frame and his hands started to tremble. He felt something unexplained and unexpected – fear.

'Something's wrong … I can feel it. Jade … something's wrong.' He stared down at the floor, clasping his clammy hands together to try to control the shaking. Sweat beaded his forehead and the tendons on his neck tensed. He felt rooted to the spot. Something inside him had sounded a warning and triggered his fight-or-flight reflex, but he felt powerless to do either.

Jade couldn't hear him over the Egyptian music belting out of the PA; her gaze was firmly fixed on the stage, intrigued by what was to come.

A bare-foot woman, draped in a loose white linen dress, tiptoed onto the stage like a ballet dancer, and then sat cross-legged on a black velour box that had miraculously appeared from behind the curtain. Braids of ebony hair cascaded over her shoulders, ending just above a crescent-shaped gold necklace adorned with turquoise and silver. Heavy makeup surrounded beautiful almond eyes that stared off into space, seeming to take in everything and nothing at the same time. A cloud of silence descended on the crowd, who sat open-mouthed, in awe of the woman's sheer stage presence.

Williams appeared at the edge of the stage, still dressed in his charcoal pinstripe suit and black roll-neck. His heavy silver necklace, ending in a large Sanskrit Om symbol, glittered and sparkled in the amber lamps, darting bright highlights against the ceiling.

'Welcome back, my friends. Now I offer you a very special guest. All the way from the ancient city of Alexandria, and for the first time ever on stage, I bring you Princess Amunet. She sees all; she knows all.' He threw something at the princess's feet; it cracked and burst into billowing plumes of white smoke that caused an outbreak of coughing and spluttering from the front row.

Pleased with the effect of his dramatic smoke bomb, Williams continued. 'She will answer any questions you have about your past or future. But be warned, ladies and gentlemen, you may not like the answers you receive.'

A crack of thunder burst through the PA system, and the audience jumped as one.

Turner stared into space, trying to figure out what was happening to him. It felt like there was a voice in his head trying to warn him about something, but he couldn't hear it no matter how hard he tried. Over the years, he'd learnt to trust his psychic sixth sense; it had saved his skin more than once. For the first time, he felt helpless to act on its warning and he tried in vain to slow his breathing and regain some control.

'Behold,' Williams said, moving to the left side of the sitting princess. 'I bring you pages from the *Book of Thoth*.' He removed a curled brown papyrus from his inside pocket and held it up with a flourish, pointing to the patchwork of hieroglyphs littering the page. 'Written here is the secret knowledge of the ancients.'

He reached behind the curtain and pulled out a white photographic tray, a bottle of beer and a flat-bottomed glass with a handle in the shape of an ankh. After laying the photographic tray at the front of the stage, he slowly unfurled the papyrus and placed it inside. Dark beer foamed from the small bottle onto the page as he gently poured at arm's length, making sure not to overfill the shallow tray. The hieroglyphs began to dissolve, streaming wraithlike as they merged with the beer.

'These secrets have brought untold wisdom to those with the gift to use them.' Williams gestured back to the princess, who sat bolt upright like a linen-clad marble statue. 'But be warned, ladies and gentlemen, these words can also bring untold horrors to the fakers and the uninitiated. Please do not try this at home.'

A few tense giggles surfaced from the back, as if the crowd were not quite sure whether his remarks had been tongue in cheek. Williams tipped the tray carefully and poured the contents into the glass with the ankh handle, the muddy brown liquor now flat and thick.

'These words have the power to bring what we know as second sight. The ability to see things unseen. To see all things that are hidden from view.'

Reverently, Williams picked up the full glass in two hands, and passed it gently to the waiting arms of the princess. Slowly, her arms raised and jangled the gold bangles on her wrists down to her elbows as she eagerly gulped down the foul-looking brew like an alcoholic with their first drink of the day. The juxtaposition of the nymph-like being's slow movements and ferocious swallowing precipitated cries of disgust and fascination in equal measure. The liquid dripped thickly from the edges of her mouth as she drained the glass, and brown stains formed on the pristine white linen dress.

Williams held up the sodden papyrus from the tray; it was now completely blank. The front row squinted in the glare and looked in wonderment at the change.

'Now she has the words of wisdom and magic inside her.'

The crowd clung to every word, fascinated by the occult nature of the performance. This was like no other clairvoyant act they'd ever seen.

Walking down from the stage and into the audience, Williams scanned for his first eager candidate.

'Now, who will be brave enough to ask something of Princess Amunet? Who wants to delve into the world of the unknown? Test her if you like. Ask her something only you know the answer to.'

As he walked down the central aisle, people leaned away, as if uncertain of this style of spiritual show. The first half had been comfortable, familiar territory that they'd experienced many times before. But this was something darker, more alien and unnerving. Unfazed, Williams continued searching. He needed someone to break the deadlock and he knew exactly what type of person to look for.

'You, sir, I believe you have a question for the princess.'

The long-haired guy with the ponytail and pierced nose stood up and grabbed the microphone, watched excitedly by his goth girlfriend with the shiny boots.

'Yeah, I've got a question, Princess.'

The guy chewed gum loudly, trying to look cool. Everything about the way he stood looked as though he were itching for a fight.

'What have I got in my pocketsez?' he squeaked out in a hiss, trying to mimic the hapless Gollum from *The Lord of the Rings.*

Half the crowd laughed, while the other half tut-tutted at this rude young thug.

'Ryan Jones.' The sound of his own name singing from the mouth of the princess stopped him in mid-chew, freezing his pierced features. 'You have a lottery ticket with the numbers four, fifteen, twenty-three, thirty-nine, forty-two and forty-five. The last number is the age your father was when he died. You always choose these numbers.'

There was no need to ask whether she was correct; his open mouth said it all. Trying to recover some of his coolness, Ponytail said, 'Okay, but will this ticket win?' He fixed an arrogant smirk back on his face that didn't quite work.

'No, Ryan Jones, it will not.'

Not sure what else to do, Ponytail sat back down, his five minutes of fame leaving him deflated. Next to him, Shiny Boots tried to console him. His only response was to spit his chewing gum onto the floor in an attempt to regain some of his rebellious street cred. That didn't work either, as an old dear poked him in the back and told him to dispose of it properly. Still playing the part of the non-conformist, he picked it up, put it straight back in his mouth, and smiled back at the shocked pensioner.

After this vulgar young man had been dealt with so easily, the audience grew in confidence and began to relax again. One of the lacy bohemian types jumped up across the room and Williams hastily scuttled over and handed her the microphone.

'Erm ... yes ... I mean, hello ... yes, I have a question, please.'

The contrast between the hesitant good manners of this stocky brunette and her predecessor could not have been more marked. Ponytail glowered sulkily at her through the gloom, blew a bubble with his chewing gum and popped it loudly.

'Erm ... well, my husband passed away last week, and, well ... I was just wondering if he's okay.'

Princess Amunet rolled her eyes and tilted back her braided head as if asking a silent question to an invisible friend. Her voice, lilting and consoling, drifted across like a gentle melody wafting through a summer meadow. 'Mr Doyle says he's fine, Norah; he has no pain anymore. Oh, and remember to take that book he was reading back to the library. He doesn't want you to be fined.'

The bohemian gasped and covered her wide mouth with a dainty hand.

Four seats away, the movement drew Turner's eye, and for the first time he looked across to the beautiful figure seated on the stage. The warning voice in his head became louder – it drifted on the tide of his mind and pulled at his memories, but he could make no sense of it. Rubbing his temples vigorously, he tried to clear his thoughts and concentrate. Death and danger clawed their way into his consciousness.

Instinctively, Turner jolted to his feet, causing Williams to hang his shoulders like a guilty man heading for the gallows.

The last thing Williams needed right now was for Turner to say something that would blow the show. Looking across, he caught Turner's eye, trying to compel him to sit back down and let him get on with it.

Turner, unsure why he'd stood in the first place, got the message and slid back into his chair, smiling an apology.

From the stage, the sight of Turner's six-foot-three frame and shock of blonde hair popping up like a jack-in-the-box and then slumping back down again attracted the amber gaze of the Egyptian beauty. But she didn't fix on Turner; she looked at the woman in the black leather jacket next to him.

'Jade,' Princess Amunet called from across the stage. 'I have your mother with me.'

Jade and Turner locked eyes, first on each other, then on Williams, and then on the white figure of the princess.

Jade glared daggers at her husband. 'Nathen, what's happening? What have you done?'

'Nothing, I swear. I don't know what's going on here. Something's not right.'

Under cover of the darkness, Jade had gone bright red, uncomfortable with the curious stares from the rest of the crowd. She'd lost her mother in childhood and the pain of her passing still lingered long in her heart.

The princess's eyes remained fixed on Jade's seated frame. 'Jade ... are you there ... can you hear me?'

Jade mouthed a yes back to the stage.

The princess's head rolled back again as if listening carefully. 'Your mother says that you're in danger.' This time her words seemed strained, the lilting tone gone, as if she were being compelled to speak. Somehow the words seemed out of sync with the movements of her mouth, like bad dubbing on a film. 'You mustn't go out alone. There's someone who wants to harm you and those you love.'

What the hell? What sort of stunt was Williams trying to pull here? thought Turner, his creeping feelings of fear replaced with confusion and frustration.

A wailing shriek pierced the air, and his blood froze as he stared in wonder at the bizarre scene unfolding on the stage. The princess appeared to be trying to wave something away with her arms as if she were fending off a horde of angry bees. She screamed again, and tumbled heavily off the velour box and onto the floor with a sickly thump. The white linen dress spread around her like a stained burial shroud as she lay still, barely breathing and with her eyes closed tight.

At the back of the room, ponytail man laughed with his girlfriend and pointed at the stage, delighted to see the graceful figure who'd embarrassed him take a fall. Others grabbed a friend's arm for reassurance, unsure of what was going on. Startled whispers echoed around the walls as greasy polo-shirt man reappeared at the edge of the stage, hastily closed the curtains, and looked worryingly across at Williams.

A brief glimmer of fear flickered across Williams's face as he tried to understand what had happened to his co-host. After taking a deep breath, he rushed back to centre stage, his gleaming white teeth smiling broadly at the crowd.

Back in performance mode, he tried to sound reassuring. 'Thank you, ladies and gentlemen. There's no need for concern. The princess had a long trip to get here and her spiritual performances are incredibly draining. We'll make sure she has plenty of rest before her next show.'

In truth, he was at a loss to explain her collapse. It looked from the outside as if she'd been wrestling with an unseen spirit, which made no sense to Williams as he was a pure sceptic where matters of the real supernatural were concerned. Faking it was one thing; this was something else, and it made his palms twitch and the hairs on the back of his neck tingle.

Noticing that all eyes were now on Jade, Williams said, 'Jade, I realise that what you've heard tonight might concern you. As I mentioned at the beginning, the answers we get from the spirit world are not to everyone's liking. We're simply the messengers. Please be my guest after the show. I'll do a free reading to dig deeper so we can understand what the message means. I'm sure it's nothing to worry about.'

Jade smiled back and nodded, not sure what else to do.

Slowly the audience began to visibly relax, looking at Williams as a caring man who'd waive his sitting fee so that one of his client's minds could be put at rest.

Bowing deeply, Williams cued his closing applause. 'I hope you enjoyed our evening together and our brief journey into the spirit world. It's been a pleasure being here and I hope to see you all again soon. Please browse through our products at the back of the room. We've got beautiful crystals, pendants and tarot cards, all at discounted prices just for tonight.'

The Lycra-clad brunette was back, waving a variety of plastic packets on a table over by the bar. She looked out of breath and flustered, but still painted a smile on her face as she swung the colourful bags around.

'Thank you, ladies and gentlemen ... and goodnight.' Williams trotted off the stage to more applause as the PA kicked in, reminding people that any claims made were not guaranteed and that the show was for entertainment purposes only.

What a pro, thought Turner, itching to get his hands around the slick scumbag's neck.

CHAPTER 4 – THE CAGED BEAR

Williams sat nervously tapping his fingers on the small desk in the backstage room of the Dancing Dog, watching Turner pace up and down like a caged bear. After asking Jade to browse the clairvoyant's pendants, cards and trinkets hawked at the back of the bar, Turner had finally got Williams on his own.

Glaring at the small weasel-like figure, now wearing a black polo shirt with red piping around the collar and a smart pair of white jeans, Turner said, 'What the hell was that? Since when does scaring my wife become entertainment?' He bounced around the cramped room, not trusting himself to sit opposite Williams. The clairvoyant would be way too close, and it would be too tempting to reach out and grab him by the throat.

Williams waved in the direction of the car park with one hand, and fiddled with the top button of his shirt with the other. 'It's nothing to do with me. It's her. Look, that stunt she pulled – it's not part of the act. I truly don't know what she was doing.'

Through the barred window, Turner could see the beaded profile of Princess Amunet, or whatever the hell her real name was, sitting in the lighted living area of a campervan. She appeared to be talking to herself.

Quickly crossing the floor and making to open the back door, Turner said, 'Well get her in then and I'll ask her myself.'

'I can't – she's meditating.'

'She's bloody what?' Turner could feel the frustration bubbling inside him, looking for a place or person to erupt over. Rarely did he lose his temper, but veiled threats directed at the person he loved most in the world had pushed him to his limit.

Williams looked down at the floor, avoiding Turner's stare of disbelief. 'Meditating. She locks herself away after a show; does some sort of talk with her spirit guide. She says she needs to do it to seek guidance and cleanse her mind.'

Flopping down in a tatty chair, Turner tried hard to release the tension in his body and regain some composure. 'Oh, for God's sake. You know as well as I do that this is a sham, so what's her game?'

For the first time, Williams looked directly at Turner, sensing that his old friend was finally calming down. 'Not to her, Nathen. She takes it all incredibly seriously. She believes in all her actions, and that her spirit guide oversees the supernatural sessions. It's some figure from ancient Egypt, apparently – she keeps a golden statue of him with her all the time. It's a bit creepy to be honest.'

Turner had to admit that he was struggling to explain how the princess had been so accurate in her stage readings, and thought that maybe she did possess some form of spiritual insight. At no point had she asked any questions to fish for clues. Her approach had been to give direct statements of fact. If the information hadn't been gathered pre-show, she must have a spiritual gift, he reasoned apprehensively. Silently, he hoped she didn't have any real divination skill as that would mean her warning to Jade needed to be taken seriously.

Looking around the room, he could see that the refurbishment efforts in the main show area hadn't made it to the back of the pub. Coarse graffiti sprawled across the bare walls, and decrepit furniture had been thrown carelessly around the room as though an incompetent interior decorator had quit halfway through. The worst of it was the smell. Stale beer, burnt cigarettes and something rotten that Turner couldn't quite place. It was like backstage areas the world over. Spend your money on the glitz and glamour out front in the public-facing areas and then have the artists get ready in a rat pit. Many times during his show days Turner had ended up changing in a cramped toilet, mastering the art of pulling on his trousers without allowing the fabric to touch the putrid floor.

Cradling his fingers together to stop them trembling, Williams said, 'I don't know her too well to be honest. I only met her a few months ago at a sideshow event down south. It seemed like she might be a good way to vary the act, so I asked her if she wanted a spot in the second half. Tonight's the first time we've worked together.'

The clairvoyant pulled himself to his feet, crossed to Turner and pushed out his hand. 'Look, I'm sorry about all this. It *is* good to see you again, Nathen. It's been a long time.'

The look on the clairvoyant's face made Turner believe

he was sorry, but he still felt that Williams was holding something back. The man looked genuinely concerned and maybe a little frightened as well. For the first time, Turner smiled and reached out to accept the offered hand.

'You too, Paul. Must be nearly four years, I guess. I thought you were still doing the magic act.'

Before Paul Wallace had changed his name by deed poll and morphed into Hugh Williams he'd been a professional magician. They'd met when Turner had dated his sister, Zoe, an unreconstructed hippy, immersed in the folk-music scene and Tibetan Buddhism. Williams had inherited a craving for being on stage from his parents. Both had been well-known figures on the theatre circuit before movies had killed off the business. Ever resourceful, his father had turned to working as an extra and effects specialist at Pinewood Studios, providing prosthetics or the appropriate amount of fake blood when required. After Williams had learnt his conjuring skills at a small but friendly magic club in Middlesbrough, he'd spent his early career performing for other magicians.

Stepping out to face the public for the first time had proved something of a culture shock. Non-magical audiences had wanted only to be entertained and had little interest in the expertise of his sleight of hand. Williams had missed the fundamental truth – a lay audience had to like you, and fiddling with cards and coins in an act more at home in a Victorian parlour show was a sure way to turn off modern spectators. His staid clichéd one-liners and sarcastic quips, aimed at embarrassing his volunteers for a cheap laugh, had literally bombed.

Studying stagecraft privately from an ex-actor and friend of the family had enabled him to hone his fake smile and turn on the charm. He'd ended up working the cruise circuit, performing on a variety of luxury liners.

Williams pulled over his chair to face Turner. 'I needed a change of identity, simple as that. I'd been doing the magic act a long time, and my agent started taking a bigger cut of the fees from my cruise work. When I confronted him about it, he basically gave me a take-it-or-leave-it deal. So I left.'

Williams fished out a cigarette and lit it, blowing wisps of blue smoke high up to the ceiling. 'Then this sod of an agent decided to blacken my reputation with all the other booking agencies, and I couldn't get any work. So, I needed to change my name, and the type of act, and now this is what I do. I thought you'd like the show – I modelled it on yours.'

Turner coughed slightly as the acrid smoke swam thickly down from the ceiling and around the room. That his old friend had based the act on his own sham performances made Turner wince inside.

'I'm out of that now,' he said. Changing the subject, he asked apprehensively, 'And how is Zoe? Is she in good health these days?'

Turner had unceremoniously dumped Williams's sibling in a tearful split one Christmas. Since then the pair had lost contact and Turner wasn't proud of how he'd behaved.

He'd met Zoe as she'd waited around to speak to him after one of his psychic shows, and the two had clicked straight away. Her spiritual view of the world and his fascination with that side of life had made them a good fit. For nearly a year they'd been inseparable, Zoe keen to learn more about the spirit world and understand how Turner tapped into it. But as their bond had grown, so had Zoe's possessiveness; she was forever flying off the handle if he as much as spoke to another woman. Trying to control a free spirit like Turner was like chasing after the wind, and he'd refused to be her puppet.

Things took a turn for the worse when her growing depression over the failure of their relationship caused a well-meaning GP to prescribe her a cocktail of anti-depressants and sleeping tablets. The chemical soup had brought on panic attacks and mild hallucinations. It became so bad that eventually her brother was forced to step in and put her into psychiatric care.

Turner had visited Zoe often, and had found her talking to imaginary friends and in a constant state of unrest, her body seemingly unable to keep still. In the end, he'd been asked to stop visiting, as her mania increased after his visits. After three months apart, she'd come home to stay with her brother, but when they'd met again Turner had felt that the bond between them had well and truly broken. He'd tried to help her heal and be there for her, but whatever had happened to her mind had made it impossible for him to keep the flame of love alive.

With a heavy heart, he'd ended the relationship. He'd never found breaking up with anyone easy, and he still felt pangs of guilt, wondering whether he should've done more to help her.

Sighing out a plume of cigarette smoke, Williams looked up and gazed out of the window, refusing to meet

Turner's eyes. 'Zoe's not bad, thanks. Better when she takes her medication, but she often forgets. I know she misses you – she hasn't had what I'd call a serious relationship since. I got her a pet to keep her company, and she dotes on it. I think having something to care for helps with her mood swings. So, yes, I guess she's as well as she can be. I see you've found love. If you don't mind me saying, your wife is very beautiful.'

None of this made Turner's guilt any easier and he regretted bringing up the subject. Going pink in the cheek, he mumbled yes and thank you and tried to steer the conversation into friendlier territory.

'I'm glad Zoe's doing okay, I really am.' Turner smiled in an attempt to convince his host of his sincerity. 'So, tell me, what's with this Hugh Williams thing? Of all the names you could've chosen – it doesn't sound very showbiz.'

Williams took a deep drag on his cigarette; smoke snaked from his mouth as he spoke. 'One of the crew on Princess Cruises told me about it and said it was a lucky name. You ever heard of a ship called the *Menai*?'

Turner shook his head.

'Well, it capsized in a gale – eighty-one passengers on board and only one survived. Guess what his name was?'

Turner shrugged.

'His name was Hugh Williams.'

'There must be hundreds of stories like that with one survivor. Why pick this one?'

The weasel face was positively beaming. 'How about the schooner that got wrecked on the Isle of Man about a hundred years after the *Menai* – sixty aboard, one survived.

The survivor was an old guy called Hugh Williams.'

'Oh, come on. You're making this up.'

Williams pulled hard on his cigarette. Smoke billowed out of his nose, dragon-like. 'Nope – check it out. There's more. Picnicking party on the Thames, run down by a coal barge, only one child survived. His name was ...'

'Hugh Williams. Okay, I get it. Enough already.' Turner was laughing now, swishing away at the cloud of smoke in front of him.

Williams reached over to grab a small hipflask from the windowsill and offered it to Turner. 'I'll drink to that – here, please, be my guest.'

Waving the leather-clad container under his nose, Turner said, 'Rum! You've got to be kidding me. Maybe I should call you Long John Hugh Williams. You're taking this naval connection a bit seriously.' He sipped gingerly at the sweet liquid, letting it ease warmly down his throat. 'But why get into the psychic scene? It's a stretch from your old finger-fiddling act.' Turner put the hipflask down and mimed a sleight-of-hand move as if he were producing playing cards from thin air.

The gesture looked more like he was knitting with invisible spider webs or having some kind of seizure, and Williams chuckled before chugging down more of the rum. Passing the booze back, he said, 'It was an accident. I took a job on one of those psychic phone lines. You know, the ones where people ring you, asking for spiritual advice.'

Turner did, but had never worked on one.

'Well, they gave me a script to use so I could handle all the usual love, travel, money and relationship questions people call in about. I'd just peddle out the usual "You have a lot of unused capacity and you tend to worry about things but try not to let your true feelings show" type of thing. Anyway, the callers swallowed it up and my job was to keep them on the line for as long as possible. The longer they were on, the more money the company made – I think they were charging £1.50 per minute at the time. But I didn't see any of that; they paid me a set fee per shift.' Glancing up to see if Turner was listening, he caught him staring out of the window, watching Princess Amunet in the campervan. 'Hey, am I boring you, Nathen?'

The braided-haired figure leant over something in front of her in the lighted living area. Slowly, she cradled a golden statue in her hands and lifted it to her forehead. It was difficult to tell from afar, but it looked like she was praying.

Williams tugged on Turner's wrist and said, 'Hey, come back in the room.'

Jolting upright, Turner nodded an apology and promised he'd give his full and undivided attention to their conversation from now on. This strange Egyptian act fascinated him and he longed to talk to her and get to the bottom of what had happened in the show. He didn't feel comfortable barging in on her meditation, or whatever she was doing, so reluctantly he closed his mind to it and turned back to his seated companion.

'So, as I was saying,' Williams said, keeping eye contact with his friend to make sure he was listening, 'the psychic phone-line company was making all this money and I thought I could make more on my own doing private readings. I took the scripts, memorised them and tried my luck at a psychic fair. Bingo! The new business was born. After faking some news stories and celebrity endorsements, I managed to book a couple of stage shows, and here we are.'

Turner took another slug from the hipflask and paused, trying to think of a way to get on with why he was there. Listening to how Williams had spawned his business, of selling compassion and exploiting human misery, wasn't making him feel any better. Deciding that the straightforward approach was his best bet, he said, 'Oh, I see.' Then he launched in directly. 'I'm not here to catch up though. I was asked to come and see the show. Do you know a widow called Mrs Craggs?'

Williams plucked at invisible dust on his shirt, took a long drink from the flask and went pink. 'Erm … maybe. She a friend of yours?'

'Not exactly. But I know you've been fleecing her for cash – I need it to stop.' Turner's jolly mood evaporated as he looked across at the squirming clairvoyant. He'd made a promise to Molly Craggs and felt honour-bound to see it through. The fact that he knew the man involved made it easier. 'There's no point denying it. I know what you've been up to. Her daughter, Molly, told me the whole thing.'

Williams's eyes looked everywhere except Turner. With a shaking hand, he lit another cigarette from the smoking butt of the first one. 'It's just business, Nathen. I meant no harm.'

Years ago, Turner would've said exactly the same thing, but now he had no sympathy for the man. How often, he wondered, did human beings use the excuse of business to justify cruelty?

'Like I said, I need it to stop. I don't want you going anywhere near her again. Her daughter reckons you've taken her for about two thousand pounds already. That's enough, don't you think?'

'But … but … you were one of us. What happened to you?' Williams was white and seemed to have forgotten the lit cigarette in his hand; it swung sideways, burning his fingers.

Turner's face was a hard, unemotional mask staring back at the twitching figure in the chair. 'You either run from things or you face them. I know who I was, but I'm not that person anymore. Things have changed and I've faced them head on.'

Having never attempted to stop anyone doing a psychic scam before, Turner had no idea how to approach it. Hoping that Williams would accept his hard line without becoming aggressive or too defensive, he pressed on. After all, the two men had been good friends in the past, enjoying many a late evening together around the crowded streets of Whitby.

'I want you to leave Mrs Craggs alone. Let her mourn in her own way.'

Silence swallowed the room, clothed in the fading blue mist of the cigarette smoke. Turner wondered if he'd pushed his point too far, so he relaxed in his chair and took a deep, calming breath.

Slowly pulling on his nicotine fix, Williams looked hard at his old friend. Inside, he felt no remorse for what he'd done. All he'd offered was comfort and closure to a grieving widow, and she'd thanked him for it. He'd never met the interfering daughter who'd brought Turner to his door and he hoped he never would. Regaining his confidence, he gazed pleasantly back at Turner and nodded. 'Okay, I'll leave her alone. But all I did was help her come to terms with her loss.'

If looks could kill, Williams would've been a sprawling heap of blubber on the floor as Turner's eyes bored through him.

Backing up from the icy stare, Williams said, 'Why is this so important to you? Are you friends with these people or something?'

Truthfully, Turner wasn't sure. Maybe it was Williams's indifference that reminded Turner of the man he'd used to be. A man he'd left far behind, never to be unearthed again. He'd made a promise to a stranger – Molly Craggs – to help, for no other reason than he'd been unable to refuse the formidable woman. Now he was here, sitting across from the scamming clairvoyant, and the lack of any regret in his old friend pricked his frustration button again. This man had to pay for what he'd done.

Deciding that hitting him in the wallet would be the best punishment, Turner said, 'And I want her money back. Every last penny you've scammed.'

Williams looked like a rabbit caught in the headlights of a truck that seemed intent on smashing him to a pulp. This was not the same easy-going guy he'd laughed and hung around with – something had changed in Turner. There was an inner strength, a presence about him that was otherworldly. Like a spiritual force had been trapped inside a lanky frame with a penchant for wearing Hawaiian shirts.

Seeing the transformation unnerved Williams. It felt as if he were looking at someone completely different but who had the appearance of a person he'd known. Figuring that Mrs Craggs must be an old friend of Turner's, or some distant relative of the family, he sat fidgeting as he tried to figure out what he should do. If he didn't give the money back, would Turner expose him as a fraud and destroy everything he'd built up? It certainly seemed possible given his friend's current state of mind. Business had been good and it wasn't like he was desperate for the cash. The recent run of stage shows had already netted him close to a small fortune.

Switching back on the charm, he said, 'Of course, Nathen. I didn't know she was a friend of yours.' He still didn't but had presumed as much. 'Come and see me tomorrow. I'll have your money. Be good to catch up on old times. No harm done, eh?'

The words seemed empty, emotionless, cold even. Williams thrust out his hand again and Turner shook it; the palm felt clammy, cold as it pressed into his, in contrast to the earlier warm handshake.

Williams scribbled down an address and plot number on the back of one of his business cards. 'I'm renting a static caravan over at Hunmanby while I do the shows. I've got a private reading booked tomorrow morning, but I'll be free about lunchtime. You can't miss the caravan; the scooter will be next to it.' Forcing a smile back on his face, he pointed to the shiny Lambretta parked outside the window.

Immersed in the mod culture and music scene since his teens, Williams had followed bands like The Small Faces, The Who and later on The Jam (once they'd thrown off their punk label) at gigs around the country. The clairvoyant had lived through a period of high fashion, where everyone expressed their individuality by dressing the same, and he still clung to the lifestyle. The scooter had always been his chosen mode of transport and he tried to get a new one every few years.

Turner said his goodbyes and wandered down the narrow corridor to find Jade waiting impatiently for him at the pub entrance.

Grabbing him by the wrist, she said, 'Well, did you get an answer? What was that whole danger-warning stuff about, and why did that Egyptian weirdo bring my mother into it?'

Before he had time to answer, the slim frame of Molly Craggs came running across the car park outside. She'd spotted Turner's lanky frame silhouetted in the doorway. Panting heavily, she said, 'Is he a fake? I was right, wasn't I? Thieving scammer.' She wasn't the kind of person who would politely wait her turn for answers and the thought that she'd interrupted Jade never occurred to her.

Nonplussed by the rapid-fire questions from two females in no mood to wait for convoluted explanations, the best Turner could do was nod at Molly.

Inside the lighted campervan at the other end of the car park, the shadowed figure of Princess Amunet seemed to be staring at him, probably finding Turner's bemusement at his situation highly entertaining.

'Right, that's it. I'm going to give that con man a piece of my mind! I've been waiting outside for you all night so I can get the news straight away. Strike while the iron's hot, that's what I say. He's not going to know what's hit him.' Molly pushed rudely past Turner, before realising she hadn't got the faintest idea where she'd find the clairvoyant, or her prey as he was now.

'Wait, Molly, wait ... *please*,' Turner called after her as she pounced from door to door, flinging them open carelessly in her hot pursuit of Williams. 'It's all sorted out, plus I've got your mother's money back. At least I will have tomorrow. He'll never bother you again, I promise. Please just come back and let me handle it.'

Spinning on her heel like an angry ballerina, Molly turned to face him. 'You've got my mother's money back? All of it?'

He nodded. What came next took him completely by surprise. Beaming happily, Molly sprinted and hugged him like a long-lost lover, pushing him out the door and into the car park in her enthusiasm.

Seeing her husband thrusting his arms out in a desperate attempt not to hug Molly back was too much for Jade and she roared with laughter.

After an awkward parting that caused another fit of giggles from his wife, Molly deftly kissed Turner on the cheek and thanked him.

After promising to bring her the money the next evening, Turner watched Molly practically skip across the car park and get in her car.

As Turner climbed rather awkwardly into the confines of Jade's Mini, he thought he saw a large shadow emerge from the other side of the street and bound behind the retreating lights of Molly's car. He rubbed his eyes to clear them and looked again. The shadow was like a large black dog that seemed hell bent on out-running the speeding motor. 'Jade – do you see that? The black dog running in the road?'

Jade peered into the blackness. 'Nope, you're imagining

things again. Get in. It's getting cold in here.'

As Jade started firing questions at him about the stage performance, the unease he'd felt when he'd first seen the nymph-like Egyptian on stage began gnawing at Turner's gut like some rabid beast.

He knew something was desperately wrong; he just didn't know what.

CHAPTER 5 – RELICS FROM THE PAST

Back at Turner's house, while he was having a heart to heart with Williams, a bizarre scene unfolded in his lounge. A petite ebony-haired Australian beauty was engrossed in sorting a variety of dirty rocks on a squat table, while her boyfriend sat strumming a slow blues tune to a large blue-eyed dog.

The normally blonde-haired Sandra Vaughan had taken a part-time gig helping at Whitby's bi-annual goth festival, and the raven-headed look was the result. Leaning over the rubble carelessly scattered across a dirty towel laid on the table, she peered intensely through a magnifying glass, turning the rocks lightly in her fingers like a jeweller examining a precious diamond.

'Hey, Lee – I've got another devil's toenail. Come and have a look.' Sandra held the two-inch stub in the air and waved it at the guitarist across the room.

Lee Melone eased past the panting pooch at his feet in a couple of long strides and peered at what looked like a contorted black-and-grey finger joint made of stone.

Pointing at the striped bands that cut into the stone's humped profile, Sandra said, 'See the growth bands on the back? Fascinating, isn't it? That's six of these beauties I've found now – I could maybe get ten pounds for the lot.' She waved her hands over the others neatly arranged in a row on the table.

Lee didn't share the enthusiasm and grunted before returning to serenade the dog.

Sandra had taken up fossil hunting along the littered beaches of the east coast, selling her haul to the boutique shop, Jurassic Jack, in Grape Lane, only five minutes' walk away from the house.

Jack Reynolds, long-time owner and confirmed bachelor, knew everything there was to know about fossils. As an ardent Indiana Jones fan he could usually be found in his shop, peering through guidebooks, planning the next big adventure, dressed in his customary khaki trousers and open-necked shirt. Jack had travelled the world and trekked through the remotest parts of Canada, China and Australia in search of his rocky quarry. Over a casual conversation in the bar Sandra worked at, pulling pints for an assorted band of regulars, she'd mentioned her financial troubles to Jack. Ever keen to help a maiden in distress, Jack had suggested she take up fossil hunting, and offered to buy the best examples from her to sell on in his shop. So Indiana Sandra was born and she'd been making a reasonable amount of extra cash over the past few months from her ancient haul.

'C'mon, Lee. This is interesting. You're looking at history here.' Sandra tried in vain to get his attention.

The guitarist just grunted again and continued to strum as the dog wagged his tail, enjoying the music. Kyle, the half Siberian husky, half Rottweiler, belonged to Turner, and along with Lee and Sandra shared the tall terraced house in Prospect Place.

'Okay, what about this? Do you know they used to powder these fossils and use them to treat joint pain?'

Lee leaned over, filled his empty glass with a large slug of Crown Royal whisky and grunted again. Lee was silently praying that Turner would get home soon and give him a break from the fossilised history lesson. Turner was his oldest friend and they'd been through everything together, sharing the best and worst of times. Often, they were mistaken for brothers, so close was the bond between them.

After Lee had finished touring with his band, the Hep Cats, he'd become the road manager for Turner's fake psychic shows, taking a reasonable cut of the purse. Things had been good for a while until Turner stopped doing the shows and moved into the psychic-coaching business, leaving Lee effectively high and dry with no income. Now he spent his days picking up the odd gig as a session guitarist or part-time roadie for local bands. After an all-day session in a recording studio in York, he was tired and grumpy.

Sensing his downtrodden mood, Sandra eased up from the table and slinked sexily across the room, moving her hips in time to his playing. Stroking her fingers gently across his fading black T-shirt, she whispered in his ear, 'Maybe if you take an interest in my *hard* rocks you might get a Jurassic *poke* later.' She kissed him lightly on the cheek.

Lee had to laugh at his Australian girlfriend and long-time love of his life. It had taken him a while to adjust from her blonde look to the sultry ebony beauty that snuggled next to him now, but it was growing on him. 'Okay,

I'm sorry. Please, tell me all about it.'

Without the music, Kyle lost interest and headed over to the fire, toasting his shaggy paws in the warm glow.

For the best part of an hour, Sandra talked excitedly about finding ammonites like coiled snakes on the tidal beaches of Whitby, and the local legend of how some thought they'd been formed when the Abbess of Whitby drove a plague of snakes over the cliff. Then on to devil's thunderbolts, the long thin belemnites formed from ancient squid-like creatures, and her favourite find – a dinosaur footprint discovered at Burniston Bay near Scarborough. She was launching into a monologue on plant remains when the front door rattled downstairs and the footsteps of Jade and Turner could be heard padding up to the landing.

Thank God, thought Lee, pulling on his third drink since the lecture had begun.

Turner burst through the lounge door. 'I'm telling you, he knows nothing about it and I believe him.' Turner stopped short, spotting the couple huddled on the couch, wondering if he'd entered at an intimate moment. He moved to head back out, muttering sorry, but Lee was already at his elbow, pulling him to a chair.

'Sit, Nathen, sit ... *please*,' Lee said, looking at his housemate with desperation in his eyes. 'Where've you been?' Lee poured Turner a generous glass of whisky to hold him a while.

Jade scanned the rocks on the table, and Sandra, needing no further prompting, pounced on the opportunity to explain what they were.

Turner looked at the pair and smiled. They were both

hunched excitedly over the table. From the back, with their ebony hair cut the same, and sporting similar outfits, they looked like twins separated at birth.

With the girls suitably engrossed, Turner lowered his voice so as not to be overheard.

'You remember Paul Wallace?' Turner eased into a lounge chair, feeling the soft embrace of the deep cushion moulding to his body.

Lee pushed his upper teeth over his lower lip in an eek-eek gesture. 'You mean Paul the rat-faced boy?'

Or weasel, thought Turner – both summed up the rodent-like scammer. 'Yep, that's him. I've been to see his show tonight, except now he's changed his name to Hugh Williams.'

Lee shook his head. 'You're kidding me, right? That man doesn't need a name change, he needs extensive plastic surgery.'

Gagging on his drink, Turner grinned and nodded in agreement.

Remembering Turner's break-up with Zoe, Lee said, 'What are you doing hooking up with him after that stuff with his sister?'

Lee had never liked the tripped-out hippy sibling, seeing her not so much as having a screw loose but more as a raving, unstable lunatic who'd been obsessed with Turner. Plus, he saw Paul Wallace/Hugh Williams as a guy with a piggy bank where his heart should be, always looking for any opportunity to make money no matter who he had to step on to get it. Definitely not people he'd want back in his life, and he said as much to Turner.

'Okay, I'll call him Hugh Williams, but I still don't trust him. Is he still doing those card tricks? You know, he took me for a small fortune in a poker game using that fancy sleight of hand of his. That man has a black belt in deceit – he's the most convincing liar I've ever known.'

'He's not that bad. We were quite close in the day.' Turner downed his drink and Lee poured him another. 'Now he's pretending to be a clairvoyant and working with this weird Egyptian act, plus at least one ringer feeding him pre-show information.'

Lee raised his eyebrows and leant closer. With his friend drinking as heavily as this, it could mean only one thing – trouble. From his time helping on Turner's old shows, Lee knew exactly what he meant about the pre-show information. The ringers, as Turner had called them, were usually friends or relatives who'd gather information for the spiritual worker to use in the show and who could be trusted never to give away this particular ruse.

'So what're you not telling me?'

Grabbing a small cigar off the table, Lee sat back and puffed at it gently, looking like a psychiatrist listening to a patient.

'Well, Hugh Williams is basically doing my old psychic show, and has rebadged it as a demonstration of clairvoyance. It's uncomfortable to watch, to be honest. I can't believe I used to be like that.' Turner thought back to all the years he'd pulled the same stunts and felt unclean. 'That's not it though, really. Like I said, he's working with this creepy Egyptian act that I can't quite figure out. I know it's not right somehow … I can't explain how.'

Aromatic smoke curled around Lee's fingers as he looked down at the growing stalk of ash clinging to the cigar. He'd grown to trust Turner's feelings over the years; his friend's ability to sense things others couldn't verged on the uncanny. 'So your spidey sense is tingling, eh? What exactly happened to switch it on?'

Turner smiled at the comic-book reference to Spider-man, one of his favourite heroes from Marvel's Golden Age. Lee had a way of grounding him and finding humour in the darkest of places.

'Well, this Egyptian woman said she was in touch with Jade's mother and passed on a message that Jade was in danger.'

Running a hand roughly through his hair, Lee shook his head, wondering what had got into his friend. 'Oh, come on! You don't believe all that stuff surely, knowing what you do about the scams that get pulled.'

'It's not that, Lee. Just before she said anything I heard a voice in my head, like someone was trying to tell me something. Warn me maybe, I don't know. I couldn't make out the words. The whole thing feels wrong.'

Lee went pale and the cigar dropped from his hand, scorching the wooden floor. Many spirits had haunted Turner since his first encounter with a ghost, causing him to give up his psychic con-man act for good. Confronted with the real supernatural, Turner hadn't been able to face pretending anymore, and the experiences he and his housemates had been through had nearly got them all killed. The thought that the spirit of Jade's mother was contacting Turner with some dire warning sent chills down

Lee's spine. He topped up both their glasses and sat silently, wondering what it all meant.

After what seemed like an age, Lee lowered his voice and said, 'Have you told Jade about this? How you feel, I mean.'

'No, and I'm not going to. She heard the warning from the Egyptian woman on the stage but believes it's Hugh Williams's way of getting back at me for dumping his sister. At least that's what I've told her. I'd rather keep it that way – I don't want her to start raking over old-girlfriend stories to be honest.'

Lee nodded, then remembered the smouldering cigar on the floor and popped it straight back in his mouth, puffing it back into life.

As he took another slug from his glass, Turner could feel the tension in his body ease now that he'd aired his fears out loud. 'I'm heading over to see Williams tomorrow afternoon to pick up some money he scammed from a widow ...'

What the hell? thought Lee. This conversation was getting stranger by the second. Looking across to see if his housemate was kidding him, Lee could see none of the usual telltales that he was on the end of a practical joke.

'Have you gone completely insane? What do you mean, picking up money he's scammed from a widow? What are you now, the Clint Eastwood of the psychic brigade?' Pretending his cigar was a gun, he pointed it at Turner. 'Have I read five fake fortunes today, or six? Go on, punk, make my day.'

Turner spat his drink over his shirt and roared with laughter at Lee's mimicry of the famous line from the *Dirty Harry* movies.

The two girls over at the table shrugged and smiled, seeing the two friends at it again. They were always like this. It was like watching a couple of naughty schoolboys sharing the latest dirty joke.

Wiping at the wet patches on his chest, Turner explained about Molly Craggs's visit and what he'd been asked to do.

Rubbing at the coarse stubble on his chin, Lee said, 'What part of that is what you do? And how come you've managed to get the money back? From what you've told me, Molly Craggs never asked you to do that. I know you're always first in line when someone is asking for help, but isn't this just going to create trouble all around?'

Of course his friend was right – Turner knew that. But sitting across from a smiling Williams, who'd showed no sign of remorse for his deceit, had irritated him. He'd wanted Williams to pay for his actions, and getting back the money he'd scammed from Molly's mother seemed to be the obvious way. At least it had at the time.

Trying to explain this to Lee would be more trouble than it was worth, so he said, 'It was just how things panned out. Williams offered to pay the money back.' Turner hoped the white lie would stick.

It didn't. Lee had known his housemate too long and could spot a fairy tale when he heard it. As he was about to dig deeper, Turner interrupted him.

'He's renting a caravan over at Hunmanby. I'm going over tomorrow to pick up the cash – it should be a scenic drive if nothing else.'

Topping up the glasses yet again, Lee decided to let it pass. Feeling sure he'd extract the true version of events later, he chose a different approach. Slurring his words slightly after over-indulging during his fossil lecture earlier, he said, 'That's settled then. I'll come with you. If he's up to something, I don't want you on your own with Rat-boy. If he's half as crazy as his sister, anything could happen.'

Wanting to find a way to cheer up the conversation, Lee headed for the guitar and knelt down next to Kyle. He beckoned Turner to watch, and slowly started picking out a mournful blues melody, bending and vibrating the strings to make it sound like a human voice lilting through the air.

The hairy hound cocked open an eye and sniffed the air. Slowly but surely, his tail began to wag along in time with the music.

Turner laughed, his creeping feelings of fear now starting to fade as he sat back and listened to the music.

CHAPTER 6 – THE CLAIRVOYANT CARAVAN

The following morning, Turner woke in a cold sweat as the dawn light streamed in through the windows of his bedroom. He'd been dreaming of a decrepit lady in a black dress, hobbling along a misty path, carrying a wicker basket. As she stumbled along, leaning heavily on a cane, Turner had seen himself offer to help carry her load. She'd willingly agreed and invited him to look at the contents. As he'd watched himself open the basket slowly in his dream, he'd screamed as he'd looked down at the severed head of Jade staring back at him with cold, dead eyes.

Trying to clear the memory of the dream from his mind, he moved quietly across the room, away from the snoozing figure of Jade, pushed open the bedroom door and headed downstairs. Splashing cold water on his face from the kitchen sink, he gazed out the window, wondering what it could mean. None of this made any sense to him but he knew something was wrong. His head was still thick from the after-effects of the whisky from the night before, and he dreaded to think what state Lee would be in. Exhausted after the emotional drain of his experience at the clairvoyant show, he and Jade had headed to bed, leaving Lee drinking and playing his guitar while Sandra snuggled in next to him.

After Turner had gulped down his fourth green tea of the morning in a desperate attempt to rehydrate his desiccated body, Lee appeared squinting from the bottom of the stairs.

Lee stretched his arms above his head and yawned. Scratching at his body like some sort of flea-ridden gorilla, he said, 'Morning,' in a dry, cracked voice that sounded like his tongue was stuck to the roof of his mouth. After downing a glass of water, he scratched his head as if thinking.

'You know, I still don't understand how you've got involved in this stuff. This is not you. I mean, you wouldn't have liked it if someone had done this to you in the bad old days.'

Lee refilled his glass with water and then started throwing bacon and eggs into a frying pan.

Turner nodded and immediately wished he hadn't. The motion caused his head to pound, and his temples throbbed like a particularly enthusiastic marching band was using them as a drum kit.

Looking at Lee with bloodshot eyes, he said, 'I know – I didn't want to do it. But Molly Craggs is not exactly an easy woman to say no to. You'll see what I mean if you meet her. Anyway, it will all be over soon. Once I've seen Williams and got the money, all I've got to do is return it to her. Job done.'

Motioning down at the frying pan, Lee asked if Turner wanted some of the food swilling about in the sizzling grease. When the answer came back as a most definite no and Turner had turned slightly green in the cheek, Lee shrugged and bundled the slippery mixture into a bread bun.

Tucking into his bacon and egg sandwich, Lee mumbled between mouthfuls, 'And what about this princess woman?'

Turner refilled his mug from the glass teapot and took a refreshing slurp. 'As far as I can see, she has nothing to do with Williams's scam. Maybe I overreacted. If I'm honest, I found her a bit creepy, so it's probably best to leave her well alone.'

'Good,' said Lee, before wolfing down the rest of his sandwich.

Turner thought back to the linen-clad figure on the stage and remembered the strange feelings that had spread through him. Had he imagined the voice in his head trying to speak to him? Now, in the cold light of day, his emotions were running cooler, as he tried to shrug off the fear from the previous evening. Hearing voices in his head was nothing new to Turner, but usually the messages were clear and easy to understand. And then there was the dream that had woken him with a start.

Unsure what else to do or say, he headed for the cupboard to grab some cereal and take in his first food of the morning.

Three hours later they were showered and refreshed, and in the silver VW Golf they shared, trundling along the coast road towards Hunmanby. A sea fret veiled the landscape, covering the fields and towns like a wispy cotton-wool shroud. They were singing along loudly to a range of blues classics belting from the stereo.

Sandra had laughed at the state of the pair before heading off on another fossil hunt near Whitby's East

Harbour. After trying to explain how it was a perfect time for it due to the tides, she'd given up, as they weren't in a fit state to receive information.

Jade had stayed back to look after Kyle, so they were two men on the road, enjoying their brief escape from the ladies.

Pulling into the caravan park brought back memories of his youth for Turner. Many times, he and his parents had holidayed at parks like this in the North East. Somehow the park seemed smaller than he'd expected. He'd found this a lot when he revisited childhood haunts – they always seemed less imposing than he remembered.

They passed the red-brick club advertising the obligatory Bingo night, and slowed down over the many speed bumps, eagerly scanning either side for any sign of Williams's scooter. After turning past the odd touring caravan and a couple of tents bravely flapping in the morning breeze, they spotted it tucked away next to a large static caravan up on a hill. Lee parked the car as close to the caravan as he could get, almost touching the raised front window. The curtains were open and a dull light from inside cast yellow rays across the front bonnet as they climbed out and headed up onto the raised decking that led to the front door.

Williams had already heard the car crunching over the gravel drive that led up to the plot, and opened the front door with a grin. Dressed in a striped boating blazer, he looked like he was about to head out on a regatta for the rich and famous. He ushered the pair into the wide living room, flicked the switch for the kettle and offered them a slightly soggy digestive biscuit. Keeping things fresh and dry inside the metal-framed home was always difficult unless it was sealed in an airtight container or cocooned in cling film.

The living room table was draped in a purple velveteen cloth, littered with tarot cards; a crystal ball sat centrally on a wooden stand. On the side windowsill, a sheaf of astrological charts and readings spread across the width of the caravan. Some had fallen haphazardly onto the foam seating below. Turner and Lee brushed aside the papers and sat down.

Opening his arms like he was accepting applause from a crowd, Williams said, 'Boys, it's great to see you.' The huge grin remained fixed on his face, bleached teeth glinting in the light from above. 'How have you been? It must be four years or so. Are you still with that wild Australian chick, Lee?'

Turner had to love the man's style. Here he was, ready to hand over thousands of pounds after his scam had been rumbled, and he'd greeted them like he'd invited them to a party. He seemed relaxed, almost pleased with himself.

Accepting a cup of black coffee in a cheap mug, Lee nodded, riled by the wild Australian chic line.

Turner spotted Lee's temper on the rise and picked up one of the astrological readings as a distraction. 'You doing charts now, Hugh?' he asked, scanning the birth chart for Libra. Without waiting for an answer, he started reading the text underneath a circular diagram littered with planetary signs. After headlining with the person's name and place and time of birth handwritten at the top, it read:

Libra
Rising sign 02 degrees Sagittarius
In your life, you have passed through many challenges, but events in the near future will bring you great happiness. You must learn to recognise opportunity when it comes and not let it slip through your fingers. By nature, you can be very trusting, but a recent disappointment has made you more critical of others. Sometimes you feel you must disguise your true feelings, but don't bottle things up as it will not help you in the long run – talk things through with those close to you. Occasionally you feel trapped or anxious, perhaps in your home or work life, and you can become quite restless. Your perseverance to overcome the challenges facing you will pay off shortly.

Sun is 16 degrees Libra
You crave the respect and admiration of others and can become irritated if you feel talked down to. Although at times you can be very sociable, occasionally you prefer to be left alone with your own thoughts. You seek an attractive home and pleasant surroundings, and are always looking for ways to improve where you live and your quality of life. Sometimes you feel your life is out of control but, given time, you will always seek practical solutions to the issues you face. You have a great deal of unused capacity and you feel you have a lot more to offer in both your work and home roles. Occasionally you wonder if you have made the right decisions in your life but you need to keep focused on the future and not the past ...

And so it went on, with the locations of other celestial bodies like the Moon, Mercury, Venus and Mars, and more personality insights written underneath.

Turner waved the paper at Williams and said, 'Do people seriously pay for these things? All this blurb could apply to anybody.' He passed the page to Lee so he could take a look.

'Exactly! Check them out – all the readings are the same. I just change the star sign, rising planets and degrees on the computer.' Williams seemed pleased with himself. 'They're lifted from a few astrology readings in the newspapers. People love them. I ask them to score how accurate the reading is out of ten, and I've never had one lower than a seven.'

Flicking through a few of the others, supposedly for completely different star signs and different people, Turner found the exact same wording on each one. Looking at the clairvoyant with cold eyes, he threw the papers carelessly onto the table.

Williams waved a hand as if to dismiss his visitor's scepticism. 'C'mon Nathen, you know the score. What's the problem? I get thirty quid a time for these.' He tidied up the discarded readings and placed them neatly back on the windowsill, smoothing out the corners; Turner's reckless handling had creased a few of them.

He moved next to Turner and sat close, crowding his personal space. Looking him straight in the eye, he said, 'You, of all people, know exactly how this game works. Astrology readings are a great money-spinner and a perfect keepsake after the clairvoyant readings.'

Grunting non-committedly, Turner scanned the room for any further evidence of Williams's cash-fleecing. All he spotted was a neatly typeset sign above the gas fire. In swirling black type it showed an extract from the Bible, quoting 1 Corinthians 14:3, about the power of prophecy to bring comfort and strength. Disgusted at this particular marketing ploy, Turner dug his nails into his thigh before trusting himself to speak. 'And business is booming, I suppose? You don't have any problems selling the private readings, even though you're stuck in this caravan?'

Williams looked less like a cat who'd got the cream and more like one who'd found the dairy.

'Quite the opposite. The site is full of holidaymakers looking for something to do. After I put up an advert in the site office the bookings came flooding in. It's easy pickings to be honest.' Unconsciously glancing across at the Bible quote, he said, 'The traditional religions have been preaching life after death for centuries. It's been repeated so often, in so many cultures, that the idea is now embedded in our DNA. But you know as well as I do that modern society, wrapped in the trappings of cold hard science, doesn't speak the same language as the old religions anymore. It's no longer enough for people to accept anecdotes written in old texts as proof that these things happened. The public demand some form of spiritual evidence, and they're losing their faith and moving away from the church. Filling this spiritual gap in their soul is exactly where I fit in. I think there's more of a demand for it now than when you were doing it.'

Williams looked at his visitors, hoping for nods of agreement. All he got back were blank stares.

He shuffled closer to his guests. 'Look, all I do is restore some spiritual belief and provide a glimpse into a secret world that offers proof of life after death.'

More blank stares as the two fellow couch dwellers remained immobile.

Still trying to explain what he thought was the blindingly obvious, Williams picked up one of the astrology charts and pointed at it. 'These astrology readings give my clients something to take home to remember their experience. Usually they'll show them to their friends and then they become clients as well. Nobody has ever complained. Quite the opposite in fact – it's very rewarding bringing comfort to the bereaved. None of my clients feel cheated.'

The two visitors looked at each other and read what the other was thinking. Both felt contaminated, as if being close to Williams had somehow corrupted them with a virus.

Their continuing silence made Williams uncomfortable and he over-talked, vainly trying to explain that he was a thoroughly good and upstanding guy with his heart in the right place. Of course he conned his clients, but for him the ends more than justified the means. He felt good about what he did for a living and it had proved a much more rewarding career, both at a personal and at a financial level, than his old magic act. He'd even thought that Turner might be proud of him and the professional way he managed his business. After all, he'd modelled his entire approach on his friend's old psychic act. But it was a different Nathen Turner who sat in front of him now – one that looked at Williams like he was some kind of demonic force concealed in a smart blazer.

Trying to ignore the disapproving glances, he spoke directly to Turner. 'C'mon, we're all friends here; you've worked in the psychic industry long enough. Everybody has a dead person upstairs they want to talk to. It's not logical; it's just human nature. People feel guilty after someone they care about passes away – have they done enough? Why didn't they spend more time with the departed? All those kinds of questions clutter their heads and they feel a need to reach out, speak to their loved ones in the afterlife and get some form of closure. They demand it even. I help people get that closure. So, if I have to lie and make stuff up, where's the harm?'

Turner had heard enough. Williams was way too close to the guy he'd once been. Hearing the same excuses he'd told himself about his past work made him feel nauseous. Wanting to move things along and get back on the road as quickly as possible, he bluntly asked for the money Williams had promised.

The clairvoyant reached in a kitchen cupboard for a black briefcase; he turned the combination lock and flicked it open. Pulling out a purple envelope, exactly the same as the ones from the show the previous evening, he handed the sealed package over with a smile. It still had 'Messages to a friend' typed on the outside and Turner wondered if this was meant to be some kind of cynical joke. He slipped it in the breast pocket of his Hawaiian shirt and stood to leave after offering a begrudging thank you.

Williams still had a broad smile on his face, unfazed by the coldness of his guests. In his profession, a thick skin came as a mandatory requirement. Waving them off, he said, 'Let's not be strangers. Keep in touch.'

The two friends literally jumped in the car like they were escaping from a bank heist. Not sure what to make of their encounter, they sat in silence until they approached Whitby

Abbey and looked out into the bay. The sight of their home town seemed to lift their spirits as they took in the red roofs tucked together like discarded Lego bricks on the east side. The sea fret was long gone and afternoon sunlight bathed the town in an amber glow as it readied itself for the holidaymakers heading out for their seaside entertainment.

Turner looked across at Lee and sighed. 'Tell me the truth, Lee, was I ever as bad as that? Williams, I mean.'

Keeping his eyes on the road, Lee paused before he answered. After a while, he simply said, 'No ... you were much worse.' He crunched through the gears straight-faced as the car headed down the steep slope into town.

Chuckling, Turner felt some of the gloom lifting from him. Lee's sense of humour always found a way to lighten the blackest of moods. The ringing of his mobile phone interrupted his thoughts. The screen showed 'number withheld'. He didn't normally answer these calls as they were usually some stranger offering him double-glazing or a chance to reduce his utility bills. On an impulse, he pressed the green answer button and held it to his ear.

'Nathen, that you? It's Tony, Tony Coppenger.'

Tony was one of Lee's friends and a long-time fan of his old band, the Hep Cats. He'd been a desk sergeant with the local constabulary for years before passing his inspector exams and moving to CID about ten months ago. Why he'd rung Turner and not Lee was a complete mystery.

'Hey, Tony. Lee's driving, but I can pass a message on.'

At the other end of the line there was a slight cough, as if Tony felt uncomfortable with the conversation. 'No, Nathen, it's you I'm after. We're trying to trace the movements of Molly Craggs over the last twenty-four hours and your name came up. Have you seen her?'

'Yes. I talked with her yesterday morning. She visited my house. Why are you asking?'

'Can you come in to the police station as soon as possible, please? Ask for me at the desk.'

In the background it sounded like Tony shuffled through papers, and police sirens wailed faintly.

'Why?' Turner asked again, wondering what the hell all this was about.

The normally cheery voice of DI Tony Coppenger was replaced with the serious tone he used for police interrogations. 'Molly Craggs has been attacked and stabbed. Her neighbour found her in her flat this morning. We need you to come in, Nathen. Now.'

CHAPTER 7 - MOMENTS IN TIME

As the two friends were making their way to meet Hugh Williams at his caravan in Hunmanby, Sandra Vaughan was chipping away at rocks underneath the cliffs near Whitby's East Harbour. She'd been combing the beach since low tide, looking for more ancient relics to add to her haul. Already she'd found a couple of beautiful ammonites and was softly whistling a happy tune to herself as she stumbled over the sharp rocks beneath the cliffs.

This stretch of coastline had proved a magnet for amateur geologists, some even willing to risk their lives climbing the shale and mudstone cliffs, looking for more elusive finds. Frayed blue ropes dangled here and there like bizarre washing lines, the lasting remnants of this dangerous hobby. Those brave or crazy enough to try the climb often got into difficulty, the knife-like rocks higher up easily cutting the nylon lines.

Sandra contented herself browsing at the bottom, turning over stones and poking at the ancient mud deposits lined in dark bands amid the vertical slopes of the cliff-side. Occasionally she'd find jet, the fossilised tree remains that had put Whitby's jewellery business on the map in the

Victorian era. Although not as lucrative as it had once been, it still made her a few pounds at Jurassic Jack's store

Jack always took pleasure in reviewing her finds and helping her identify some of the less obvious ones. His own personal collection amounted to thousands of assorted ancient remnants and he was particularly proud of his hoard of Whitby snakestones. Jack had explained to her that cunning dealers in the nineteenth century had carved snake heads on the larger ammonites and sold them as relics of St Hilda, who, according to legend, had turned Whitby's snakes into coils of stone. If nothing else, the snakestones provided a great story for the purchasers to pass on during dark nights huddled around the fire. Jack loved telling this story to tourists and had managed to sell quite a few in the process.

Sandra's access to this particular stretch of fossil-rich beach had come after a long walk through the town towards the East Harbour. After passing the old fishermen's houses and white-fronted shops crammed with holiday trinkets, a short climb up the cobbled street had wafted the unmistakeable smell of smoked kippers past her. The smokehouse, nestled on the corner of a narrow street, had been a famous feature of the town for over a century. Passing the heady aroma of wood smoke and seeing the fish dangling temptingly in the window, she'd felt hungry and had regretted skipping her breakfast in her enthusiasm to start the hunt. After a quick search in her shoulder bag had unearthed a chocolate snack, she'd munched her way down the steep path that plunged to the shore. From past experience, she knew she'd have to time her visit just right. The turning tide had a habit of trapping the unwary against the cliffs, from which a dangerous climb over the rocks provided the only escape route. After carefully timing her visit that morning, she was determined to maximise her stay on the beach, searching for her stony quarry.

She knelt down and began tapping at a piece of loose shale with her short pick. The blows sent shockwaves down her arms; her wrists were already aching from her morning's work. After several minutes, the dull rock sheared along a central seam. Excited, she peeled back the top to find about half a dozen small ammonites curled in their rocky grave. She reached into her shoulder bag and pulled out a plastic bottle with a tube poking from the top. Slowly, she squeezed the sides of the bottle, causing droplets of water to spread across the surface of the shale. The water always helped to enhance the impressions as well as clear away fine dust, and after examining it minutely with the magnifier around her neck, she was pleased to find that the fossil was even better than she'd first thought. The whole process fascinated her. It opened up a moment in time captured in rock – a view of an ancient land when strange and wonderful creatures had roamed the earth, long before humanity arrived to rule the planet.

A crash in the distance made her look up. A small figure shrieked and fell limply, probably from one of the blue lines anchored high in the cliff. Sandra thrust her find quickly in her bag and raced towards the scene. Slipping and sliding over the loose shingle, she headed down to the sand where it was easier to run. She looked around; the rest of the beach was empty. The morning sea fret had kept people safely snuggled indoors rather than braving the freezing mist. Her boots squelched in the sand, leaving watery imprints as she raced on, and then she zigzagged back up to the cliffs.

Panting heavily, she knelt next to the prone figure lying face down in the dirt. Even close up she couldn't tell whether it was a man or a woman – the back of the head and hair were covered by a woolly hat. Stained cargo trousers, mottled with sand, topped a pair of ankle-high boots that looked like they'd seen a lot of wear. To the right, among the rocks, lay a bamboo walking stick and a small canvas bag.

She pulled carefully at the black fleece covering the torso and slowly turned the figure on its back. What she saw made her recoil and cover her mouth. The lower part of the face was covered with a bizarre mask, like those used by people spraying toxic paint, but this one was thicker and made of flesh-coloured material. Drawn on the fabric was a pair of smiling ruby lips in a gentle grin. Assuming the mask was there to shield the wearer from the inevitable fragments of rock dust that came from chipping away at the cliffs, Sandra took a deep breath and mentally chastised herself for backing up. Why the owner had decided to paint a pair of lips on it was a mystery. Perhaps a sign of a warped sense of fun, she thought, relaxing. Fossil hunting attracted a lot of colourful characters with unusual habits, but she'd never seen anyone decorate a mask in this way. Vampire fangs, yes, given the town's connection with the Dracula myth, but not a set of chops more at home on Marilyn Monroe. The figure remained unresponsive, and Sandra moved closer, ready to remove the mask and check for signs of breathing.

As she got nearer, the figure's eyes flicked open and stared at her. Heavy folds of skin under the lower lids gave the visible parts of the face an unnerving appearance.

Stopping mid-stride, Sandra said, 'Hi, are you okay? I heard you fall.' Looking up at the cliff face, she could see a blue line swaying in the breeze, and assumed that was where the stranger had been climbing. Sandra offered a tentative smile at the masked figure.

No answer, just a slow blink of the eyes above the painted lips.

Thinking that the fossil hunter might be concussed, she tried again. 'Do you feel okay? You've had a nasty fall. Can I help you?'

This time the figure offered a slow nod, pushed against the cold rock underneath and sat upright. The masked head shook from side to side and said, 'What happened?'

The voice spoke with a lisp but was definitely feminine. At least that was one mystery solved, thought Sandra. She'd guessed female, given the mask design, but it wasn't always a sure thing these days. 'You fell. I don't know how far – I heard you rather than saw you. I was over there, near those boulders.' She pointed back down the beach over her shoulder.

Nodding as if finally understanding, the figure started wiping rock dust and sand from her top. The dirty gloves she wore simply added to the debris, so she gave up in the end. 'Can you help me to my feet, please?'

Between them they struggled on the slippery ground, falling into each other a couple of times and giggling before eventually they made it. The woman motioned towards the bamboo walking cane and Sandra picked it up and passed it over.

The woman leant heavily on the stick, made her way to the mouth of a small cave carved by the sea into the foot of the cliff and sat down. Standing over her, Sandra didn't know quite what to make of this unusual visitor to the shore. She'd certainly never seen her before and was about to ask her how often she came here, when the women's voice interrupted her musing.

'Tell me, dear, do you think I'm pretty?' The voice had changed to a higher pitch with a grating tone, like nails scraping down a blackboard, and the lisp had got worse.

Sandra looked around and began to step backwards, wondering what the hell she'd got herself into. If this was some female sex pest seeking a mate, then she was most definitely barking up the wrong tree. From inside the cave mouth, Sandra would be invisible to any passers-by on the beach. She needed to get out in the open if this lady did indeed turn out to be a weirdo.

The woman reached up from the floor and grabbed Sandra's retreating ankle with a strength that belied her small stature. Still holding on, she sat up, keeping her eyes locked on Sandra. There was something in those eyes. They were gleaming, glittering with excitement in the morning light bathing the entrance. This was getting way too creepy for the petite Australian and she renewed her efforts to pull away, more frantically this time. Beads of sweat began to break out on her forehead as she tried in vain to escape the vice-like grip.

Time began to slow down for Sandra, like she was waking up from a particularly deep sleep. Everything appeared to happen in slow motion as the figure reached up to remove the mask.

Gazing now – face to unmasked face – the androgynous figure said, 'How about now? Do you think I'm pretty?'

Sandra screamed and drifted into blackness.

CHAPTER 8 – QUESTIONS AND NO ANSWERS

Turner sat slumped in the cheap plastic chair opposite the uniformed sergeant. He'd been stuck in this white-walled interview room for over an hour and felt claustrophobic. The worst part was the smell. Whatever dregs of humanity had previously occupied the small space had left a lingering reminder of their presence. Something like a cross between a public toilet and a dog's armpit made him wrinkle his nose and try to breathe in as little as he could.

After dropping Lee at the house, he'd made straight for the police station as DI Tony Coppenger had demanded. From his first step into the building he'd felt uncomfortable. After standing in line amid a colourful group of youths waiting to be questioned, he'd found out that Tony had been sent home early as he'd been asked to cover the night shift. From behind a scratched glass screen, the officer had offered a brief apology about being short-handed, and an assurance that someone would be with him shortly.

Turner had looked around for somewhere to sit, then squeezed himself onto a bench between two thugs with menace in their eyes. The rest of the group standing around the cramped waiting area hadn't helped his nerves either.

One woman, her skirt up to her armpits, had leant in a corner, chewing gum and blowing bubbles that burst with a soggy pop. Two men in tracksuit bottoms and baggy T-shirts had been loudly cursing anything and everything to do with the police. Grey T-shirt man had said to red T-shirt man, 'I can't believe they're keeping us waiting. Don't they know we pay their wages? Bloody police.' And on it had gone, with a string of four-letter words to drive the point home.

Turner had felt guilty just being there. Sitting with as neutral an expression as he could muster, he'd stared off into space, desperately trying not to make eye contact with anyone. The seated thug on his left had leant over, pointed and said, 'Nice shirt, pal.' His breath had smelled of cigarettes and stale beer and the nail on his index finger was yellow and mired with dirt.

For probably the only time in his life, Turner had questioned his preference for loud Hawaiian shirts and had simply nodded in reply.

Not satisfied, the thug had grinned and continued, 'But you do look like a dick, pal.' His eyes had stared into Turner's, pleading with him to argue back or start trouble.

'Turner? Nathen Turner? Through here, please,' a uniformed officer had called from a connecting door.

Turner had shot up like a cork from a champagne bottle and run across the room to the waiting officer. The relief had faded to misery again when he was greeted by the stench in the interview room.

Over the past hour he must've confirmed his name, date of birth and address about fifty times. At least that was how it felt to him. He still didn't know exactly what had happened to Molly Craggs. They wouldn't tell him – they were asking *him* to tell *them* all about it. Which was impossible, as he had no idea.

The smart uniformed officer scanned over the clipboard, reading her handwritten notes again. Over the past decade, she'd seen it all. With romantic dreams in her head, she'd joined the force with the expectation of fighting major crime and bringing justice to the masses, like a modern-day Batgirl swathed in a police uniform. Reality had proved somewhat different; she spent the majority of her time settling violent domestic disputes, tackling people with mental-health problems or trying to talk down the odd suicide case. Looking at Turner in his crazy Hawaiian shirt, she assumed she was back to dealing with a mental-health problem.

Wearily, she said, 'So you're saying Molly Craggs called on you yesterday to ask you to go to a clairvoyant show. And you'd never met her before that day. You also say that she didn't want to go to the show herself and yet she met you in the car park after it.' Saying it out loud seemed to confirm her suspicion that this guy was mentally deranged.

As she read it back, even Turner thought it sounded made up. Out of professional courtesy or moral compass, he didn't want to say that he'd gone to the show to expose a fake clairvoyant. He had nothing personal against Williams and, frankly, had never wanted to get involved in the first place. He could imagine the headlines, 'Spiritual swindler exposed by one of his own', and that certainly wouldn't do him, or Williams, any good.

Realising he hadn't replied yet, he said, 'Yes, that's right.'

Raising her eyebrows, the officer grunted in reply and

continued scanning down the page. 'And you're saying that you have two thousand pounds belonging to Molly Craggs – sorry, belonging to her mother – that you'd like to return?' Her eyes scanned the lanky figure. Yes, she was definitely dealing with another fruitcake.

Oh, crap, thought Turner. This was getting worse; panic started to rise inside him. Underneath the table, his knee bounced up and down like it was having its own epileptic fit. 'Yes, that's right as well. As it turned out, the clairvoyant was a friend of Molly Craggs's mother and he owed her the money. He gave it to me to return as I think he's moving out of town for the next week or so with his shows.' Turner hoped his lies would stick and satisfy the officer. The jumping knee was getting worse, so he ran a hand down his trouser leg, trying to hold it steady.

Watching the twitching psychic, the officer assumed he was coming down after imbibing some illegal substance. From past experience, she knew it would be impossible to prove as most drug addicts had an uncanny knack of hiding their stash. Rather than press her suspicion further, she offered another non-committal grunt and stared at him, allowing silence to fill the room – the one used by newspaper journalists the world over when interviewing politicians. She knew that something in the interviewees' heads would make them crave to fill the gap, and they'd often say something they shouldn't.

Turner could hear a youth swearing and banging on a wall outside, and then there was the sound of a scuffle. Feeling like he'd entered some sort of parallel anarchic universe, he attempted to calm the feelings of guilt growing inside him. After all, he knew he hadn't done anything, though it didn't sound clear-cut from his statement. Still searching for information about what had happened to Molly Craggs, he tried asking. So far it had been a one-way process of him answering the same questions phrased in a multitude of different ways.

'Can you please tell me what's happened to Molly Craggs? All I know is she's been stabbed.'

'And how, precisely, do you *know* she's been stabbed, Mr Turner?' The officer sat bolt upright, finally feeling she was on the scent of the truth.

Oh crap, thought Turner again, the twitching returning to his limbs. 'Erm ... they told me on the phone. DI Coppenger told me. I mean, is she okay?'

The officer seemed to peer through him before she looked down and scribbled a few notes. 'DI Coppenger told you, did he? Well, I'll have to ask him about that. I'm afraid I'm not allowed to tell you any more at this stage. Is there anything else you'd like to add to your statement?'

Deflated, and not trusting himself to pursue things further without digging a bigger hole for his already dubious position, he shook his head.

'Okay, Mr Turner, sign here,' she said, passing him a pen and motioning towards the foot of the page. 'I'd like to take a DNA sample from you. Any objections?'

Turner said no, and she removed a cotton-wool swab from a plastic bag. She stuck it in his mouth and swiped it down the inside of his cheek. After a 'thank you' and 'we'll be in touch,' Turner left, tracing the dry part inside his cheek with his tongue and heading as fast as he could for the car.

He drove home in silence, wondering what was going on. Things were starting to get very weird, very quickly. All he knew from the detective's phone call was that Molly Craggs had been stabbed and found by a neighbour. He had no idea if she was dead or if she'd said anything to the police about him. The one thing he'd not realised from watching crime drama on TV was how intimidating a police station could be in real life. After five minutes inside, he'd felt as though he could confess to anything.

Lee and Jade were waiting for him at the kitchen table when he arrived back home. He filled them in on the little he knew and the process he'd been through, and was just starting to relax when there was a banging on the front door. The kitchen served as the front room of the house, the large oak door opening directly into the street beyond.

Turner yanked the door open, about to berate the visitor for their rudeness, but stopped short. DI Tony Coppenger stood on the doorstep, and this didn't look like a social call.

Tony's Jamaican parents had moved to the UK in the sixties, enticed by the prospect of regular work.

Clothed in a well-made grey suit, black shirt and bright red, gold and green striped tie, Tony still had the look of a Rastafarian who'd been forced to get a haircut and conform to this particular dress code. His shirt rippled tightly over his biceps and large chest; he'd been a keen rugby player in his youth.

Forcing a smile at Turner, he asked politely if he could come inside.

'I've been into the station already, Tony, and given a statement. You didn't need to call. Anyway, they told me you were on nights.' Turner was exasperated; he'd seen more than enough police officers for one day.

Tony looked downtrodden, heartbroken even. 'I'm not here about Molly Craggs, Nathen. I need to see Lee – it's urgent. A body's been washed up on the beach near the east cliffs, and I think it might be Sandra Vaughan.'

CHAPTER 9 – SORROW ON THE SANDS

Lee stood alone on Whitby's East Pier, gazing out to sea. To his right, the sea crashed against the rocky shoreline pushing fountains of spray high in the air. He moved to stand close to the salty jets, allowing the foaming surf to splash over his body, soaking his clothing. He was cold and wet, but he simply didn't care. Looking down, he could see the stone pillars in dire need of repair; evidence of their battering by all the North Sea could throw at them lay in the crumbling stone at his feet. Lee hoped they'd collapse and swallow him up, and then drag him out to sea, never to be seen again.

A couple of tourists had laughed at him and pointed at his bedraggled appearance, like he was some kind of a freak in a carnival show. Lee hadn't even noticed. He was immersed in a world of sorrow, like living in a bad dream that he couldn't wake from. He feel helpless and alone as the cold salt spray prickled his face.

Earlier, he'd stood gazing at the pale face of the one he loved, lying still and barely breathing in the critical-care unit at Scarborough Hospital. Sandra Vaughan had looked for all the world like she was sleeping, but the white cotton sheets, pulled up tight to her neck, and her mottled bruised face told a different story. Her corpse-like body had been found on the shoreline off the East Cliff flats that afternoon. The mussel-encrusted beach had torn at her skin as the waves rocked it mercilessly back and forth, covering her body in hundreds of cuts and slashing her clothing.

Thankfully, the hospital staff had covered up the damage and tucked the bedding in tight around Sandra's slim frame to shield Lee from the worst of it. Behind the bed, multiple machines had blinked silently, lit up like the cockpit of an aeroplane. The myriad tubes and wires draping down from the machines disappeared under the bedding or were taped to various parts of his girlfriend's body. An oxygen tank hissed air into a mask strapped across Sandra's nose and mouth. Lee held her hand, tears streaming down his face.

A consultant in a green gown and somebody called a Bereavement Officer had pulled him aside and taken him into a narrow, soulless room lined with purple vinyl chairs. After taking down Sandra's personal details and information on her living relatives, they'd explained the situation as kindly as they could. Sandra had a large puncture wound in her stomach and she'd lost a lot of blood. They'd spoken of her survival in percentage terms and estimated around five per cent if she made it through the next twenty-four hours. Lee must prepare himself for the worst, they'd said, as he'd grunted back monosyllabic answers, trying in vain to hold back his tears.

After that, there'd been a trip in a speeding squad car to Whitby Police Station where he'd sat in front of Tony and answered questions.

It was all a blur in his mind, and he struggled to believe

that the pale, inert figure in the hospital was his girlfriend.

The best the policeman could tell him was that Sandra appeared to have slipped heavily on the jagged rocks during her fossil-hunting expedition, and the incoming tide had washed her down the beach.

Lee couldn't take it all in and didn't want to go home and face more questions from his housemates. Plus, at the house, Sandra's things would surround him. He wasn't ready to be reminded that she wasn't there, that she was fighting a battle for her life, that she'd most likely lose, and that there was nothing he could do to help. It couldn't be true, he thought, still struggling with the nightmare that had taken over his life.

So there he stood, watching the waves, the aqueous evil of nature that had most likely killed his girlfriend. He slumped down, cradled his knees and rocked back and forth. The light faded as the sun sunk behind the cliffs, bathing the water in a blood-red glow. He stared vacantly at the surf; the hissing and crashing of the waves pounded in his head. As the tears flowed like a river down his cheeks and merged with the wet stone below, all he could think about was Sandra's battered frame on the hospital trolley.

Across town, Turner sat in front of a woman pouring out sorrowful tears of her own. After Lee had been called away by Tony, Turner had needed a distraction; he hadn't wanted to think about what Lee might be going through and hoped it wasn't bad news. He'd headed off to find Molly's mother, and now he sat listening to the news about the attack, at a loss to understand who'd want to do such a thing.

Turner pulled out the envelope containing the two thousand pounds and passed it to Jessica Craggs. The resemblance between mother and daughter was uncanny; both shared the same sharp features. Turner sat apprehensively in case the parent shared the same fiery manner.

Easing back in his chair, he spoke softly in an attempt to imbue the room with a sense of calm. 'This is the money the clairvoyant guy swindled from you. Your daughter asked me to help, and I got your money back.' He smiled, hoping the money would somehow put a stop to the crying. It didn't; it just made it worse.

Jessica wiped her face self-consciously and smeared her makeup. 'She was such a kind child, always thinking of others. I'd no idea she'd come to see you. But I guess that was her way of helping. Since Jim, my husband, died we've all been at sixes and sevens. Then this stranger shows up with a message from beyond the grave ... and now this ...' She grabbed another tissue from a box on the table and loudly blew her nose.

This was becoming too much for Turner. He didn't even know this woman and here she was, tearing her heart out in front of him. Looking for a way to break the atmosphere, he offered to make a pot of tea and hunted for the kitchen without waiting for an answer.

The small bungalow was a two-room affair, bedroom and living space, with a kitchen in between. The house had been easy to find among the scattering of retirement properties on the outskirts of town. It was a small community and a few polite door-to-door enquiries had led him straight there.

After a quick rummage through the kitchen cupboards, he found a couple of mugs and a teapot and set about making a strong brew.

When he returned, Jessica looked brighter and cradled a framed photo of Molly in her lap. Pouring out the tea, he looked at the smiling face in her hands and wondered again what on earth had happened to her. Chancing his luck, he asked as politely as he could.

Jessica took a deep breath, sipped at her tea with a nod of thanks and for the first time made eye contact . 'She was found in her flat by a neighbour. Stabbed – just lying on the floor in a pool of blood. No sign of a break-in and nothing stolen. It seemed like whoever did it was only interested in harming her, nothing else. They say she died quickly.'

Dead? Turner rubbed his palms together and wiped at the cold sweat on his forehead. He felt – no, it was more than that – he knew this death was somehow linked to him. Whether it was pure intuition or a more supernatural hunch, he couldn't say. But the sense of connection was real, or at least it was to him.

Jessica continued, 'Whatever killed her wasn't a normal knife. They said it had a rectangular blade, around three quarters of an inch wide, and it pierced all the way through her chest, like a sword, I suppose.' She started sobbing again and Turner passed her the now half-empty box of tissues.

Not knowing what else to do, he sat in silence as she tried to compose herself. A large carriage clock, seated centrally on the marble fireplace, ticked away the time, minute after minute. Two Chinese-style ornamental dogs gazed down at him unemotionally from either side of the clock, oblivious to the atmosphere of heartache and sorrow in the cramped space. The air was heavy with the scent of lavender from a plug-in air freshener in the corner, but a lingering mustiness clung to him. He silently hoped he'd never end up living in a house like this. There'd been more space in the static caravan he'd visited that morning, and it seemed too small a box to live in while life ebbed away. Another loud snort to clear blocked sinuses interrupted his thoughts.

Pulling herself upright and sipping at her tea, Jessica looked across at him through the steam rising from her cup. 'I don't think they were supposed to tell me how she died, but I insisted. My only daughter – and they wanted to play cloak-and-dagger stuff with me. No, sir, that's not what we do in this family.'

Turner recognised the same stubborn, and rather intimidating nature, he'd seen in her daughter. He'd need to tread carefully and make sure nothing he did or said provoked this grieving widow. How the now-deceased husband had coped with two such strong women, he had no idea. Turner felt he'd be a quivering wreck within a week of their company.

'Do they have any idea who's responsible?' he asked, somewhat weakly.

Jessica shook her head. 'Of course not. They never do, do they?' She seemed to be paying more attention to her houseguest now, as if sizing him up. Slowly, her gaze lasered over him, from the battered cowboy boots to the collar on his colourful shirt. Tilting her head like a bird listening for a worm, she tapped the purple envelope containing the cash gently on the table. Her internal musings over, she passed the envelope across to Turner and said, 'I want you to find out. Take this for your trouble.'

Turner held back, not sure what she meant.

She pushed the envelope deep into his palm and closed his fingers around it. 'I've never met you, Nathen Turner, but I've certainly heard of you. You're a psychic, right? A real one, not like the charlatan that came to my door.'

What now? thought Turner, unsure how to respond. It was true that he had a genuine connection with the supernatural, but his days of working with clients as their psychic adviser were long gone. He'd faked his ability back then anyway, and certainly didn't want to go anywhere near that world again. In his mind, he didn't see why having his particular spiritual talents compelled him to share them with others in that way. Certainly, spirits came to him for help, but it was sporadic and often took him into dangerous situations he'd rather avoid. His spiritual journey had moved him into coaching others who thought they had a gift, not offering potential life-changing advice to a group of strangers. The connection with the spirit world haunted his days; if he could, he'd turn it off and live a completely different life – a normal life that was full of everyday matters rather than otherworldly problems.

Reluctantly, Turner nodded and tried to give her back the money. He was not in any position to deny his past and felt trapped into the admission.

Smiling across at him, Jessica said, 'I knew you were. A girl who works in the salon where I get my hair done comes to you for psychic coaching. She can't say enough good things about you. I can tell you're different somehow; you do have a certain style.'

Probably the shirt, thought Turner, looking down at the flowery monstrosity. Glancing around the room for a possible escape route, he pushed himself to the edge of his chair and placed the envelope with the cash onto the table between them.

As he tried to stand and make as polite an exit as he could, Jessica grabbed his arm. 'I want you to use your psychic skills to find the killer. If you can really sense and see things that others can't, you should be able to do it. I want you to make contact with Molly's spirit and find out what happened.'

'But—'

Jessica held his arm and his gaze, challenging him. 'But nothing. If you're the real deal this should be easy for you. Or are you just another con man after all?'

Turner was not having much success saying no to any woman with the surname Craggs. Once again, he was being pushed to do something he didn't want to do. It was like sitting opposite a primal force that would destroy anything in its path. No wonder the police had given her the details of Molly's brutal death. They'd likely felt the same – say no and she'll eat you for breakfast, and then snack on the rest of your family for afters.

Whether he could help, he genuinely didn't know. Regaining some composure, he said, 'Look, I don't know if I can help and I certainly don't want your money.' He picked up the envelope and gave it back to her. She accepted it without any further drama. 'If I'm to try, I'll need something of hers. Something personal that she treasured. An object that her spirit might feel drawn to.'

From past experience, Turner knew that someone's keepsake, or an item they'd cherished, would provide his best chance of contacting their spirit in whatever part of the afterlife they'd ended up. This territory was much more familiar to him, but the chances of it having any success were usually between slim and none.

Heading to the sideboard, Jessica pulled out a gold cross on a narrow chain from the top drawer. The yellow metal gleamed in the light from the window, making Turner squint.

'Here,' said Jessica. 'The police gave this back to me. Molly wore it around her neck all the time.' She fumbled with a small hidden clasp on the side of the cross and opened it up. Inside the shallow chamber were a few strands of dark wispy hair. 'That's a lock from her first haircut as a child. She always kept it, and thought it would bring her good luck.' She began to sob again, closed the cross, and thought about how it had brought her daughter no luck at all.

Turner accepted the cross respectfully and wrapped the gold chain around it so it occupied as small a space as possible. Then he put it in the pocket of his jeans. After not promising anything but saying he'd try his best, he headed out into the cool evening air, wondering what the hell he'd got himself into.

CHAPTER 10 – STRANGE BREW

Once home, Turner had sat up all night, waiting for Lee to return with any news on Sandra. Jade stayed with him until about three in the morning but had given up when her body could no longer stay awake. As the sun rose across the bay, trying vainly to spread its light through the cloud cover, there'd still been no sign of Lee, and he wasn't answering his mobile. It was the same story with Tony – he was now off-duty and the police remained tight-lipped about the body they'd found on the shore.

With nothing else to go on, Turner catnapped for an hour, then showered and shaved before heading out with Kyle towards Tate Hill beach. Since the tightening of the local by-laws he couldn't let the dog roam free on his favoured West Cliff beach, with its vast expanse of sand and surf, so the smaller stretch at Tate Hill was their go-to haunt. Kyle hated the confines of a lead, and Turner was in no mood to try and rein him in that morning.

As he wandered up the narrow path towards the town, he spotted the familiar form of Kenny Florian washing off seagull waste from the front of his shop. Kenny owned and ran The Alchemist. It was Turner's main source of tarot cards, crystal balls and the like, and home to one of his oldest friends. The seagulls were an unnecessary evil in the seaside town – at least as far as Kenny was concerned – and the daily cleaning formed part of his morning ritual before opening the shop.

Spotting the hairy hound running towards him and the familiar lanky frame of Turner trotting behind, Kenny called him over. 'You all right, Nate? You look knackered.' Kenny refused to call him Nathen, as it simply wasn't cool enough in his hippy-obsessed worldview.

In truth, Turner was exhausted, but the cold morning air helped to revive his dulled senses. Patting Kenny on the shoulder he said, 'No, I'm okay. Just had a rough couple of days, that's all.'

Kenny pulled him and the eager pooch inside to a back room of the shop that served as a kitchen. His wife, Rosa, stood stirring a huge saucepan of something that looked disgusting and smelled foul, while she happily puffed away at an electronic cigarette wedged between her teeth. Her culinary experiments had put Turner and Kenny close to the emergency room more than once, and now they knew better than to try her latest brew.

'Just making some soup – brand-new recipe,' Rosa said between clenched teeth. 'Do you want to try some?'

Both shook their heads in unison and moved quickly to the back of the room, as far away from the bubbling pot as they could.

Rosa shrugged and continued her stirring. 'Okay, but it's your loss. The flavours should be fantastic in this one. I've added seaweed and a dead crab I found on the beach.'

Sticking the electronic cigarette behind her ear, where it teetered and looked ready to fall, she spooned some of the soup into her mouth. Smacking her lips, she said, 'Delicious', ignoring their wrinkled noses and pained expressions. Even Kyle covered his wet nose with a shaggy paw, and cowered under the kitchen table.

Kenny pulled out a couple of chairs and poured Turner a dark-looking drink from a teapot in the middle of the table. Turner raised his eyebrows at the steaming brew, and Kenny muttered, 'It's safe – just liquorice tea. She swears by it in the mornings.'

Reluctantly, Turner took a sip and found it surprisingly pleasant. In the far corner, by the back window, a gardener's tray was full to the brim with odd-shaped mushrooms. Next to it, along the windowsill, a row of unlabelled glass jars held a variety of dried things in various shades of red and brown. A taut washing line, stretched up close to the ceiling, held a couple of dead rabbits that dangled down and smelled funky. How Kenny had survived so long on the lethal diet concocted by his wife, who was obviously nose blind and possibly mildly insane, Turner had no idea.

Kenny patted Kyle and said, 'What's up, Nate? I can tell you've got something on your mind.'

Turner didn't know where to start. He felt things were wrong and that, somehow, he was at the centre of a lot of death and destruction, but he had no idea how to explain it. The best he could offer was, 'You ever heard of a clairvoyant guy called Hugh Williams?'

The shopkeeper laughed. 'Not him again. What is it about that guy? I had a fearsome woman in earlier this week asking about him. She sounded like she wanted blood; he'd conned her mother or something. She looked scary enough herself. Anyway, I sent her over to your place, as it seemed to be a supernatural swindle and in your area of expertise, not mine. I've had a few of his show flyers in the shop, but I'd never met or heard of the guy before that.' Kyle started licking Kenny's hand, braving the smell in the room and sniffing the air. 'Is that what's bothering you? You're upset with me for putting her in touch?'

'She's dead.'

Kenny stopped laughing. He could tell that Turner wasn't trying to pull some kind of sick joke from the expression on his face. He'd known his friend wouldn't be happy about the referral but hadn't known what else to suggest to the fiery lady who'd asked him for help.

Yet another man terrified of saying no to Molly Craggs.

Pulling himself upright, Turner refused a top-up of the steaming liquid in his cup. 'She was murdered yesterday in her flat. I've already been questioned about it.'

'You? Why are they questioning you?'

'I guess they need to "eliminate me from their enquiries" or whatever the hell the phrase is. It's so crazy – I only met the woman a couple of days ago, but I feel responsible somehow.' Turner scratched an invisible itch on his head, wondering if the rabbits hanging above had dropped some biting flea or other parasitic passenger onto him. Leaning away from the possible drop zone and wanting to change the subject, he said, 'This Hugh Williams guy has a weird act in his show – a woman who parades herself as an Egyptian princess. She does this bizarre kind of spooky ritual and then a psychic show. Oh, and there was someone else there doing pre-show. A slim blonde gathering information up front – do any of those two ring a bell?'

Scratching his chest, and feeling something crawling on him, Kenny thought about it and said, 'I've never heard of this princess woman but my guess is the blonde is Samantha from the RADAK Corporation.'

The Remote and Distance Activity Kit manufacturers were an underground supplier to the psychic community, providing a range of meters and electronic devices to a wide range of professionals working in the spiritual field. Turner himself had been a long-time user of their rigged ghost meters back in his scamming days. A covert button had allowed him to set off the so-called ghost meter at will and scare many of his past clientele on his spooky tours around Whitby.

Lately, RADAK had been branching out into the service arena and were offering to hire out individuals who could work covertly, and confidentially, to help psychics gather information on any potential punter. Many manifested as door-to-door salespeople who'd check out a client's house before a reading, or were experts at gathering information from the Internet. Through a wide network of dummy Facebook and other social media accounts, it was a relatively easy task for them to find complete strangers' most intimate details. Coupled with access to census information, births, deaths and marriages records, and regular scanning of local media, the service they offered was second to none.

The reputation of the psychic professionals they served was entirely dependent on the psychic/medium/clairvoyant being able to present information that they couldn't possibly know to a gullible member of the public, and RADAK were just the people to find out the apparently unknowable and meet that need.

This was the first time Turner had heard about RADAK providing pre-show staff as well. 'So, is this Samantha slim, about five foot three, with big boobs and a winning smile?' He pushed away the liquorice tea that looked like it was starting to ferment in his cup.

Kenny nodded. 'Yep, that's her. She used to be an actress – I think she still does the odd job here and there, but makes more money on the RADAK contracts. Nice girl, but she can't seem to hold onto a man for long.'

Turner wondered how much of her ability to keep a relationship was down to her chosen profession, but offered no comment.

'Anyway, enough about this Hugh Williams guy. That's not what's bothering me, Kenny. It's Lee – he's gone AWOL. I think Sandra's had an accident. The whole thing feels wrong. It's like someone's trying to destroy the people around me.'

Without thinking, Kenny looked around as if trying to spot a sniper in the shadows. Realising what he'd done, he smiled apologetically. 'I'm sure it's not as bad as that. Just a coincidence, that's all. Sandra will be fine and Lee's off on another bender. You know what he's like if he bumps into his mates.'

Turner nodded and hoped Kenny was right.

He offered his farewells and headed up the cobbled street into town, the dog running ten yards ahead, glad to be away from the stinky kitchen.

Usually, Turner would stop at the odd shop and say his good mornings to the locals or past clients. Today, he walked with his head down, lost in thought.

After about ten minutes, he cut down the sloping alley between the shops that led onto the hidden beauty of Tate Hill beach. The soft sand gave easily under his boots, causing him to slip and slide forward as Kyle dived headlong into the water and paddled happily off the shore.

Slowly, he made his way around the horseshoe-shaped beach and towards the East Pier, ignoring greetings from the odd passer-by. The overcast weather matched his mood and he kicked idly at the sand, musing things over. Would he be able to contact the spirit of Molly Craggs? he wondered, not at all confident in his ability to do what had been asked, or rather demanded of him. That was not his forte; normally the spirits came to him unbidden or a vision appeared in his dreams. He silently hoped the dream he'd had of Jade's dead head in a basket wasn't a spirit message warning him of things to come. The only time he'd deliberately tried to summon a ghost, using an ancient ceremony Jade had stumbled across, it hadn't ended well and had nearly got him killed. To even try, he knew he'd need some similar sort of ritual to call back Molly's spirit, using the gold cross her mother had given him to strengthen the connection. How others claimed they summoned spirits without tapping into ancient ceremonies and long-lost knowledge bemused him, and he felt sure they were making it all up to deceive unsuspecting clients.

Locked away securely in his room was a bewitched

crystal ball that dated back to the Elizabethan era. He'd acquired it during another ghostly adventure, but only used it to discover the history of those it had belonged too, no more. He'd need to find something different, and decided to comb through his bizarre book collection when he got back home. Even the idea of trying gave him goose bumps, so he picked up the pace, trying to warm his trembling frame. Striding along, he still wondered how the hell he'd got into this mess in the first place.

Up ahead, he spotted the forlorn figure of a tramp lying in a foetal position on top of the pier. Others were walking past, tut-tutting or confused that there was no hat or dish to accept small change and offer the wretch money for food or a hot drink.

As he got closer, he made out the wet jeans and battered leather jacket pulled in tight against the cold. A tangled mass of brown hair dripped salty water onto the stone serving as a solid pillow for the poor soul. Turner fished in his pocket for change and climbed up the rocks towards the tramp. Something made him stop short.

The clothing was familiar.

Then he sprinted forward as recognition set in like a lightning bolt through his heart. The prone figure was Lee.

CHAPTER 11 – AN INSPECTOR CALLS

Turner immediately pulled out his mobile phone and gave a few hasty instructions to Kenny back at The Alchemist. Then he knelt down to the sorry figure; Lee looked to be asleep. He was pale and breathing rapidly, almost panting.

Having spotted his owner leaving the beach, Kyle came bounding up, licked at Lee's grimy face, then recoiled at the taste of the stone dust stuck on his tongue.

Sensing the stinky drool on his face, Lee tried to sit up and open his eyes.

Turner cradled his soaking friend in his arms. His clothing was already saturated, a large damp patch spreading across his Hawaiian shirt. 'Lee, can you hear me?'

Lee murmured something in reply, but his voice was slurred as if he were drunk. There were no empty cans or bottles so Turner thought this unlikely. Up close, he could feel Lee shivering, his whole body trembling as he pulled him tighter. Turner had recognised the symptoms from his first glance at Lee. After a battering by the North Sea, the chill winds and cold spray had often left Turner's fisherman father in states like this. His friend's body temperature must have dropped and hypothermia was setting in. How extreme it was he couldn't tell yet, but he needed to get Lee back home and warmed up as soon as he could.

As consciousness returned, Lee began reaching up to unzip his jacket and remove it. Turner grabbed his hand and fastened the coat back up. Again, he'd seen this before. His father had been a partner in a small fishing vessel and in freezing states like this he'd often tried to remove his clothing. Turner had never understood why, but watching Lee confirmed his earlier diagnosis.

Kenny appeared, puffing and panting up the pier with a garish purple blanket in one hand and a thermos flask in the other. He thrust the woollen bundle at Turner and said, 'Will this do? Best I could find – it's one of our new range of table throws for tarot readings.'

Quickly, Turner wrapped his dripping friend in the purple abomination and pulled it tight around his shaking frame. At least Lee wasn't in any fit state to see what he'd been wrapped in, he thought, as he pulled him into a seated position.

Kenny poured black liquid into a cup from the thermos and held it up to Lee's pale lips, tilting it so he could take a drink.

At the taste of the steaming brew, Lee gagged. 'What the hell is that?' he said, but his words were slurred and they couldn't understand him. Thinking he asked for more, Kenny kept pouring.

This continued for about five minutes, although to Lee it felt like an eternity.

Kenny had asked his wife to make a particularly strong brew of the liquorice tea and felt certain this would be just the thing to revive the shivering guitarist. Pleased that it seemed to be stimulating Lee back to life, Kenny said, 'That's it, Lee. Get it down you. It's good stuff. I knew you'd like it.' Kenny kept pouring, muttering more words of encouragement.

Lee looked up, his eyes pleading with Turner to stop the liquorice waterboarding. Neither of the helpers read the signals and kept encouraging him to drink. So there they all sat, Lee in a purple blanket, surrounded by two people who seemed intent on drowning him with a tea that tasted like it had been made in Bertie Bassett's kitchen.

A couple of people walked past and laughed, thinking it was the aftermath of a stag party. 'Rough night, huh?'

They walked on, giggling and pointing back. Turner did his best to ignore them and supported Kenny's hand, holding the cup as he held it up to Lee's mouth.

In desperation, Lee pushed shakily to his feet, stumbling a few times. He retched on the sickly-sweet taste in his mouth, and said, 'For God's sake. Will you stop?' Wiping his dusty hand over his lips, he glared at his two helpers as they backed off, surprised by his now clear voice. The effort to stand was too much for the guitarist and he sagged again, only to be caught under the arms by Turner.

Glad that Lee seemed to be coming to his senses, Turner said, 'What happened to you? Where's Sandra? What the hell are you doing out here?' The words tumbled out as he desperately sought answers.

Too exhausted to reply, Lee slumped in Turner's arms, causing him to buckle under the weight. Deciding it would be best to leave his questions for later, Turner motioned Kenny to help him lift his frigid friend to his feet and get him back to the house.

With Turner under one arm and Kenny the other, Lee finally started moving back down the cobblestone streets towards home. The effect of the tea had turned his lips black and he looked to passers-by like some type of purple-caped goth as he tripped past the crowded shops and shuffled his way forward.

Turner ignored the sniggering and sidelong glances, fully focused on getting Lee home and next to a warm fire. He knew they'd have to take it slowly as a quick rise in his blood pressure could be fatal. So, wobbling step by step, it took them an hour to get home, stopping occasionally to rest.

Kyle padded behind, head bowed, not understanding what was going on or what had happened, but knowing he must guard the trio. He turned his shaggy head and cast threatening glances at the grinning people they passed, itching to give them a growl to shut them up.

Rather than disturb Jade, who was still snuggled fast asleep after her late-night stint with her husband, Turner and Kenny pulled Lee up to the lounge and stripped his wet clothing. They dried him as best they could, and dressed him in a pair of loose jogging bottoms and a hoody. Then they pushed him into a green sleeping bag and sat him up on the sofa.

Some of the colour returned to his face, but try as they might they couldn't get rid of the black staining on his lips. Silently hoping Lee wouldn't notice when he came to his senses, Turner busied himself lighting the fire.

'Sorry, Nate, I should get back to the shop. It's not a

good idea to leave Rosa on her own for too long,' Kenny said. 'Will you be okay with him now? You can ring me if you need anything.'

Turner nodded in reply and, satisfied that he'd done his bit, Kenny rushed back to the shop to relieve his wife.

Lee was gradually waking as if from a deep, frozen sleep. Shrugging up in the sleeping bag, he toppled over, not realising his hands and arms had been zippered inside. Turner dove across to the sofa and gently pushed him upright again, his hands shaking with the effort. 'It's okay. You're at home now. How do you feel? Can you tell me what happened? Why were you out on the pier? And where's Sandra?'

Looking around the room and realising he was back at the house, Lee stretched and felt the warmth from the fire seep into his ice-cold frame. He unzipped the sleeping bag from the inside to free his arms and pushed himself into a more comfortable position. Slowly, he began to speak, the words stammered as his body shook. 'I ... can't remember. I just can't remember.' A tear oozed from the corner of Lee's eye. Turner hugged his friend, now feeling more worried than ever.

Realising that Lee had no memory of the past few hours, Turner thought it best to explain everything that had happened after finding him on the pier.

Listening but not necessarily believing, Lee nodded occasionally into the air, trying desperately to remember.

'Look, Lee, what I'm telling you is the truth,' Turner said, wondering whether his friend needed medical attention. 'If you truly can't remember anything, then I'm taking you straight to the hospital.'

That one word – hospital – made Lee keel over like he'd been shot. Wondering what on earth was going on, Turner simply asked him.

As if struggling for breath, Lee said, 'She's there. Sandra's there – at the hospital,' and tears began to flood down his cheeks. 'I remember now. Everything ... I remember everything.'

So Turner's fears were real – something had happened to Sandra, and whatever it was had needed medical attention. More concerned than ever, Turner's words flew out in a rush. 'Well, that's settled then. We're going to the hospital and we can both call in and visit Sandra while we're there. What's happened to her? Why is she in hospital?'

As he reached over to fully unzip the sleeping bag, Lee stopped him by grabbing his wrist.

'She's dying, Nathen. I've seen her – they've moved her to critical care at Scarborough. They've told me to prepare for the worst; she's not expected to survive the next twenty-four hours. There was some sort of an accident on the beach – someone found her washed ashore and they thought she was dead already.'

Silence.

Seagulls darted past the open window, riding the air currents and twisting in the breeze, on the hunt for their next meal. Boat engines roared in the harbour, as the small vessels puttered out to sea, their owners chatting over the state of the declining fishing industry. Happy tourists rushed through the streets, eager to explore the quaint shops and tempting cafes. Normal Whitby life, going about its everyday ebb and flow. But inside that first-floor room, life would never be normal again.

Turner sank to his knees and wept, leaning against his friend's legs as Lee rested his hand gently on his housemate's shoulder. Kyle buried his face in the blanket, sensing something was dreadfully wrong. Soft sobbing filled the air and the dog began to whimper, not sure why, but feeling a compulsion from somewhere deep inside.

And so they sat, no words of consolation passing to break the silence. Each felt lost in his own grief and disbelief; waves of pain washed over them, filling the room with an ocean of sadness. Eventually, Turner stretched Lee out to sleep and took the dog downstairs, desperate to escape the air of gloom that hung in the lounge. His mind was full of questions, but one thing was clear. He must get to Scarborough Hospital as soon as possible and see Sandra for himself.

Jade found him at the kitchen table, huddled over an ice-cold mug of green tea with Kyle curled up asleep at his feet. Between sobs, Turner managed to tell his wife the news and, ever practical in times of crisis, she began firing questions at him.

'You told me yourself, Lee seems a little unbalanced at the moment. He could've got it wrong. When did this happen? Or how? What do we know? Are you sure it's her?'

On and on it went, rattling around Turner's brain until he'd finally had enough.

'Please stop. I don't know, okay?' Turner pleaded. 'But I believe him. We need to go and see her.'

Before Jade could answer and fire more questions at

him, they were interrupted by a knock on the front door. What now? Turner thought. His house seemed to be inundated with unexpected visitors at the moment and none of them brought him good news. Dragging himself to his feet and wiping at his face, he tried to put on a mask of normality – the same mask worn by doctors, fire fighters and police officers who'd witnessed untold human horrors only to be faced with the heart-rending task of telling the next of kin.

Turner pulled open the heavy door to find Tony and a uniformed officer standing there, looking at his soaking shirt and reds eyes curiously. Turner sagged, like all the air was leaking out of him. After taking a deep, calming breath, he hauled himself upright and said, 'Please, not now, Tony. Lee's just told us the news about Sandra. Can't this wait?'

Tony had his police-business face on; he apologised for bothering him again at home and asked if he could come in.

Standing by the kitchen table, he asked Turner and Jade to sit down. This didn't feel right to either one. It was like being in the presence of the grim reaper and watching him sharpening his scythe. The uniformed officer stood behind Tony, his arms behind his back, holding a stern but worried expression.

Tony reached into his suit jacket for his notebook. He flipped it open and got straight to the point, in complete contrast to his usual amiable style. 'I *am* sorry about this, Nathen, but I need to tell you something. It simply can't wait, I'm afraid – it's for your own safety.'

He asked whether Lee was at home and if he could join them. Turner said he was, but that he couldn't be disturbed. In his eyes, Lee's fragile state of mind meant he was in no fit state to talk to the police.

Tony flicked to a new page in the notebook littered with tiny handwriting. 'We've done the autopsy on Molly Craggs. The surgeon has also filled me in on Sandra Vaughan's injuries. I'm here to tell you that they were both attacked with the same weapon.'

Turner thought some drunken coroner must have done the autopsy and got his wires crossed – some of the coroners he'd come across socially were no strangers to the inside of a whisky bottle. 'But Lee told me that Sandra had an accident on the beach and was washed ashore, next to dead. How can they have been attacked with the same weapon? Molly was found stabbed in her flat, for goodness' sake.' Unconsciously, he tugged at his hair, his emotions hurtling like a rollercoaster with no brakes.

Tony looked at his uniformed colleague as if asking permission. The officer nodded. What Tony was about to tell them was not exactly by the book, as Turner was still an active suspect in the Molly Craggs murder investigation. Friendship and loyalty were driving Tony's behaviour, but he'd still brought a colleague with him as a witness in case he got hauled up in front of a disciplinary hearing. The uniformed officer was an old schoolmate who'd deny that Tony had ever passed the information on if or when it ever came to it.

Tony cleared his throat. 'They were both stabbed by a weapon that we haven't been able to identify yet. We believe Sandra was unconscious before she entered the water. It looks like the incoming tide washed her body further down the beach to the spot where she was found. There's no evidence that she was ever fully immersed – she had no seawater in her lungs. Everything points to the fact that she was attacked on the beach and then left for dead. We wouldn't normally tell you this, but ...' His cheeks went pink as he glanced down at his shiny shoes.

'Both attacked by the same weapon? Are you sure?'

Tony looked up and gazed directly at Turner. Now back in standard police-business mode and with the mask covering his true feelings firmly lodged in place, he said, 'Very sure. And it looks like the same person did it. For some reason, they appear to be targeting people you know.'

CHAPTER 12 – A LIFE IN THE BALANCE

That afternoon, the three housemates sat sullenly by the large blue doors outside Scarborough Hospital's critical-care ward. A lopsided notice warned that only two visitors were allowed per patient and that visiting times must be strictly adhered to. Turner watched the large clock on the wall tick slowly by, second by second, as if 2 p.m. would never come. Next to him, Lee sat with his head in his hands as Jade wrapped her arms around him, telling him everything would be okay.

A bleach smell wafted down the corridor every time a new visitor appeared through the huge elevator doors. Each visitor had their own mask of sorrow, doing their collective best to hide the pain inside. So wrapped up were they in their internal musings that none spoke to each other or even passed the time of day. What awaited them behind the blue doors was too much to bear and each held a silent vigil as they shuffled on the plastic fold-out seats that lined the wall.

Occasionally, a clattering steel stretcher would be whisked past and slammed through the doors, attendants running behind, shouting medical jargon at each other from their green and purple gowns. All the three housemates could do was sit and wait as the seconds crawled by.

A small grey-haired woman in a blue smock pushed open one of the doors and smiled sympathetically. She'd worked in the ward for the past five years and had seen more heartache than anyone should see in a lifetime. Having served as a military nurse, she'd found a way to close down the emotional part of her that dealt with the pain of loss and death. But the faces of the deceased still haunted her dreams – especially the children, whose innocent faces had looked at her as the flame of their brief lives had finally flickered out. Keeping her voice low and consoling she said, 'Who's first, please?'

Turner dragged Lee to his feet and moved to the door. 'We're here to see Sandra Vaughan.' They'd already agreed that Jade would stay behind first so that they didn't breach the two-visitor rule. Turner would come out later so she could head in.

Pulling Turner by the arm, the grey-haired lady ushered the pair of friends to the left, past the reception desk, and into an open-plan ward. Patients lay feet apart, their only privacy provided by a green plastic curtain supported by a rail in the ceiling. It was impossible for the pair not to look at the sorry cases that filled the beds, each one in their own private battle for life. An air of death clung to the place and filled the space with a feeling of a living graveyard. Fluorescent lights in the ceiling kept the ward lit twenty-four seven so there was no sense of day or night, just one of simple survival.

The green curtain had been pulled around Sandra's bed and they stepped through it to be at her side.

The frail figure in the linen sheets looked like she was sleeping, but a large clear bowl cocooned her head and fed oxygen from a pipe in the wall. The rack of machines, their trailing wires taped to Sandra, sat unemotionally blinking out their readings to the attending nurses. Around Sandra's abdomen, blood had seeped through from the dressing and stained the sheets. Imperceptibly the prone figure's chest rose and fell at a pace so slow that it looked as if her life were already ebbing away into the sterile surroundings.

Moving as if in a dream, Lee pulled up a chair and held the cold hand that draped over the side of the bed.

Trying desperately to keep a lid on his emotions, Turner pulled aside one of the nurses checking the machines. 'How's she doing? Have you got any more information on what happened to her?' He manoeuvred the nurse out of earshot of Lee to spare his friend the answer if it was bad news.

The nurse lifted the metal clipboard from the side of the bed and scanned the results before replying. Turner's gaze was fixed on the transparent globe around Sandra's head. As if reading his thoughts, the nurse said, 'Don't be alarmed about the oxygen helmet. We've had to move her off the facemask as her levels weren't where we wanted them to be. She's a lucky girl – the odds of her making it this far after the extent of her injuries ... well, let's just say someone's smiling down on her.'

Flicking to another sheet criss-crossed with readings and scribbled notes on medication, she looked at Turner's gaunt features before continuing. 'But she's far from out of the woods yet, I'm afraid. We've put her into a medically induced coma to allow her body to heal. As to what happened to her, I don't know. We simply treat the injuries. All I can tell you is to stay positive. With every hour, she has a better chance of coming through.' Fondling the silver crucifix around her neck as if to emphasise her words, the nurse kept her voice low as she whispered into Turner's ear and glanced at Lee. 'You must keep strong for your friend. He was in yesterday and he'll need your support. He was in a terrible state.'

Turner thanked her for her kindness, then moved to sit with Lee and pass on the news. The psychic had never been an overtly religious guy, holding to the belief that it was improbable that one faith should outrank another. Why people killed in the name of religion when the source of these ideologies preached forgiveness and peaceful co-habitation at their core left him dumbstruck. A pacifist at heart, the thought that war could be justified by aligning it to a spiritual belief made him question human psychology. He'd often wondered whether humans were genetically hard-wired to the kill-or-be-killed mentality as the species fought for survival throughout history. It would certainly explain why Homo sapiens kept building bigger and more lethal weapons to kill each other. With these doubts and questions clouding his mind, he'd kept an open mind on all religious persuasions. But tonight he'd pray. To whom he wasn't sure, but he'd plead for Sandra's survival and hope that somebody, somewhere was listening.

After saying his farewells in as optimistic a manner as he could muster, he headed outside so that Jade could visit Sandra. Now alone in the sterile corridor, he sat on the seat with his head in his hands. Deep inside, one thing kept pulling him back and demanding his attention. A feeling that pricked at his conscience and wouldn't leave him alone.

He knew that somehow this was all his fault.

CHAPTER 13 – SUMMONING THE SPIRITS

That evening, Turner sat alone in the lounge, trying to shake off the feeling of fear that haunted him. Something gnawed at his subconscious, trying and failing to settle clearly into his mind. After leaving the hospital he hadn't been able to rid himself of the sense that something or someone wanted to hurt his world, and so far they were succeeding.

During their evening meal, Jade, Lee and Turner had sat mostly in silence, unsure of the right words to say. Words didn't seem to mean anything anymore. They'd seen a person they all loved fighting for her life and none of it seemed real. Sandra had shared their dreams and their downfalls in equal measure. For her life to end like this would be tragic. But more than that, it felt like a wound that cut them to the core and made everything feel different. Things would never be the same again.

Concerned that Lee was still a flight risk, Turner made him sleep in the bedroom he shared with Jade on the top floor. That way Lee would have farther to travel and they had more chance of hearing him if he decided to go walkabout again. As an early-warning precaution, he'd also put a blanket down for Kyle to sleep on outside the bedroom door. He hoped that his boisterous hound understood the job in hand. Turner had spent ten minutes talking to him in the vain hope that some part of the message had got through to his furry head.

Realising that Turner needed time alone to take in the happenings of the past couple of days, Jade headed for Lee and Sandra's room. She'd made him promise to join her later and not stay up all night worrying.

Turner had given his word but knew he'd struggle to keep it. There was too much rattling about in his brain – thoughts and emotions twisting and turning, and none gave him any comfort.

Now alone, Turner flicked off the lights and put another log on the embers of the fire. The flames crackled and burst into life. Sparks flew as the resin in the wood simmered and oozed down the side; dancing lights popped up the chimney like tiny fireworks. Watching the spreading blaze in the darkened room soothed him. He felt like the rising flames were alive somehow, breathing new life into the lonely space. For some reason he'd never truly understood, he'd loved watching fires ever since the bonfires of his youth. There was something primal, primeval even, that captured his attention and fascinated him.

Slowly, he began to work through the events of the past few days, piece by painful piece – his meeting with Molly Craggs and being drawn into doing things he hadn't wanted to do. He thought back to the night at Hugh Williams's show. The strange fear he'd felt, and the wordless voices he'd imagined when the nymph-like princess had taken to the stage. Without thinking, he snorted in derision, his mind calling out to him, *Princess indeed. Who the hell does she think she is?* But she'd tried to warn him, or at least warn Jade. What did she know? How could she know? Had he misjudged her? Perhaps, like him, she was touched by the spirits and had an ability to sense things not of this world. There was definitely a presence about her that had connected with him in ways he simply didn't understand. He needed to find her, talk to her and get to the truth. If she turned out to be another scammer, he felt confident he'd know pretty quickly, and that would be an end to it.

The fire crackled hot sparks at his feet, breaking his train of thought. Turner stood and put the large brass fireguard in front of the growing blaze and fished in his jeans pocket for a handkerchief to tamp out the burning embers on the floor.

His fingers wrapped around the gold cross Jessica Craggs had given him. He pulled it out and looked at it reflected in the firelight. The thing looked alive, pulsing and shining in the amber glow. Jessica had asked him to contact her daughter in the spirit world and find the truth about her death. After a lifetime spent pretending he could do this, he now found that spirits wandered into his life unbidden, drawn to him like he was a kind of metaphysical magnet. Turner had somehow inadvertently opened a secret door into the supernatural that simply refused to close. He'd left behind everything that Williams did – that life of deception and working as a spiritual parasite, preying on the grief of others. All the spiritual contact he'd had since had come naturally, or with the help of old texts or artefacts he'd picked up on his travels. But these were all locked away upstairs next to the sleeping Lee. Starting a frantic search for anything that might help would only disturb his housemate, and that was not something he was prepared to do. Lee had been through enough already.

He held the glittering cross with the tips of his fingers, then turned it upright, like a cleric offering a blessing. The hidden opening catch was well disguised in the inner corner where the two beams of the cross met. Using the edge of his fingernail, he managed to gently pull it down. The cross swung apart, revealing the small chamber inside. The fine strands of wispy hair stared back at him as if to say, 'What do you want with me? Leave me alone.' In truth, he was stuck on what to do next, and how he might try to contact the spirit of Molly Craggs in his quest for answers. Without his books on the bizarre and esoteric, he'd have to try to remember something right here and now.

Sinking back on the settee, he allowed his eyes to close. Calling on an old memory trick, he imagined an ornate library spread over two floors with a winding staircase connecting them. Ironically, the technique had been taught to him by Williams, who'd used similar methods to remember the order of playing cards in a shuffled deck for his magic shows. The idea was to link memories to places and objects that could be visualised rather than try to recall things by rote and repetition. He'd heard some call these visualisations their memory palace – like a building with distinctive features, each of which could be associated with a memory. Turner's memory palace was a library filled with facts and information on the supernatural.

Gradually, he pictured himself heading up the staircase of his internal library and browsing the dusty volumes on the shelves in a hidden corner. As titles came into view, he watched his hand reach out and pick up one called *The Golden Bough*. It felt as if he were an observer in one of his dreams; he calmed his breathing and immersed himself in the picture, sensing the smell of the polished wood and the musk of the old texts. Pages flicked by, then the book dropped open at a section on hair and its taboos. He read in his imagination as the author explained the belief in sympathetic magic and how a connection was thought to exist between every part of the body, even when the physical parts had been separated. Damaging, say, a discarded fingernail or lock of hair would in turn lead to damage on the physical being of the person. A long list of examples followed but none was of any use to Turner – he didn't want to harm anyone.

He returned the volume and watched himself move down the row and pick up a work describing the Salem witch trials of the seventeenth century. His finger reached out and pointed to the name Samuel Shattock. Intrigued, he felt himself drawn closer to the text to read the small writing. The tale described how Samuel's daughter had fallen ill in 1685 and that the prescribing doctor had been convinced that the cause was witchcraft. In a bizarre ritual, they'd boiled some of the child's hair, believing the person who'd caused the illness would be summoned to the foul-smelling brew. According to the text in his mind's eye, this technique had worked and some unsuspecting witch had wandered into the dwelling, drawn by the simmering lock.

Turner's head nodded back on his chest as the visions faded; he could smell again the familiar scent of the fire.

Using memory techniques had been part of his stock-in-trade as a fake psychic medium – he'd found that throwing in the odd genuine fact did wonders for his readings. Stoking up the fire, he wondered whether any of this recalled information would be of use in his current situation. After all, he knew the Salem witch trials had been largely discredited in these more enlightened modern times. But for some reason he'd been drawn to these works; and nuggets of knowledge sourced from bizarre places had saved his life before.

Pacing around the floor, he puzzled over how he could use the knowledge dredged up from these memories of his book collection. None of the examples specifically helped him summon a spirit. But, if the suggested connections between parts of the body were correct, maybe the hair could form a sort of spiritual bridge to the soul of Molly Craggs. Thinking he'd nothing to lose, he headed downstairs to the kitchen and collected a shallow cup of water and some tongs.

Sitting in front of the fire, he felt foolish and was glad nobody was around to see what he was up to. Carefully, he pulled out one of the fine threads of hair from the hidden chamber in the cross and placed it in the cup, where it floated on the surface of the shallow water. Using the tongs, he placed the cup in the fire, wedging it in the corner so it couldn't fall over. Now what? Maybe if he concentrated on calling Molly's name in his head, it would help create a connection to her spirit as the water started to bubble and steam in the cup.

The smell was terrible, like burnt rotten eggs, and he gagged as it wafted across to him.

'Molly, come to me. Molly Craggs, I need you now. Help me, Molly,' he said in his mind.

Nothing. He tried again. Still nothing except the twisting flames that seemed to mock him. Now he felt like some irrational weirdo sitting in the firelight amid the sulphurous atmosphere. It clung to his clothing, as if he were in some brimstone boudoir.

Enough, he thought, and stood to turn on the light and go to bed.

Standing by the door, flickering in the amber light from the fire, was the wispy figure of Molly Craggs.

CHAPTER 14 – COLD SPIRIT

Despite the fire, the temperature in the room plummeted. Flames flicked forward towards the shadowy figure of Molly as if pulled by an invisible hand, and Turner began to shiver. This was old territory for him and he'd grown used to being in the presence of spirits throughout the years. Rather than fear, he felt pleased that he'd managed to make contact, and he moved closer.

He was aware that the newly passed often had difficulty the first time they reappeared in the mortal plane. Without their corporeal enclosure, their spirit often bumped into things and stumbled blindly. He'd often wondered whether this was where the legend of poltergeist activity had come from, and thought he was probably right. To manifest in a visible form took a lot of energy and was usually impossible on a first visit without some appropriate spell or ritual. His use of the hair and his own spiritual ability seemed to have been enough to summon the spirit of Molly, but the figure shimmered and faded like a reflection on water. Turner guessed he didn't have much time before it faded completely.

Speaking slowly and deliberately, he said, 'Don't be afraid, Molly. You're safe here.' Molly's last memory would've been of her brutal murder and this would be foremost in her ethereal mind. 'Your mother asked me to find out what happened to you and bring you justice. Can you help me? Will you help me?'

Turner moved within touching distance of the wispy shape. Up close, the temperature was ice cold and he could feel the sensation draining from his fingers as his breath misted the air.

The eyes of the figure seemed to look through him. The mouth began to move, but no sound came out. Frozen breath wafted from the lips and over his face, causing him to recoil. Ignoring the cold, Turner leant closer, desperate to hear anything. He watched the lips purse as if trying to force the words out.

After what seemed like an age, the figure said, 'Pretty. Do you think ... I'm pretty?' The words were hollow, like someone talking inside a steel barrel, and they felt more like they'd come from inside Turner's head.

What the hell? Having managed to summon the departed spirit, he was now being asked whether it looked good.

He tried again. 'Molly, I need you to concentrate. Can you describe what happened?' Slowly, he leant in, almost touching the outline of the shimmering face. 'Please, I need your help.'

The pale lips pursed again. 'Old lady ... walking stick ...'

Without warning, the shimmering vision reached up her cold hand and placed the open palm on his forehead. Icy water seemed to flood into Turner's brain and pictures began to form in his mind. He could see a room – her flat, he assumed – and Molly answering the door. It wasn't open wide enough for him to clearly see the caller, but he made out a glimpse of black fabric and a hand reaching in with a collecting jar with the name of a charity on the side. There was a veil over the face of the caller that reminded Turner of photographs of Victorian women in mourning. The black figure stepped inside, limping, using a bamboo cane to steady itself. He watched as Molly and the visitor appeared to have an argument, saw Molly reach up and lift the veil on the visitor's face. Then the vision faded as quickly as it had appeared.

Molly's vaporous body dissolved into a freezing mist, which coiled and drew towards the fire. Turner reached in with both hands and immediately wished he hadn't. They turned blue and went numb, causing him to gasp with pain. All he could do was watch as the vapour billowed and spread around the fire before disappearing into the flames with a hiss, like water hitting hot fat.

Turner moved to slump on the settee, feeling like a complete failure. None of this made sense. How could a lame and slightly creepy old lady swathed in black have murdered Molly Craggs? According to the police she'd been stabbed straight through the chest with some as yet unidentified sharp implement. The veiled figure in his vision hadn't seemed to have the strength to walk far, let alone subdue and kill a woman who'd no problem fighting her own corner. Molly had roped him into going to Williams's show against his will and he couldn't imagine her giving up without a confrontation that would rival the most brutal catfight.

But there was a similarity between the black figure and

the one he'd seen in his dream that worried him. The dream figure had carried Jade's severed head in a basket, and even thinking about it made him shudder.

With no other options left, he decided to grab a few hours' sleep and try again tomorrow. Something inside made him feel he needed to track down Williams and seek his help finding the mysterious Egyptian woman who'd shared the stage with him. She'd seemed to know or sense something, and had warned Jade. If she truly had a spiritual gift, maybe they could work together to bring the killer to justice.

Turner knelt by the fire and prayed for help, hoping that someone, somewhere would hear him.

As the golden rays of the dawn flooded through the lounge window, Turner stretched and bolted to his feet. In the brief time between sleep and consciousness he'd felt good; then he remembered the tragic events that clung to the house like a black fog.

Without bothering to wash or shave, he scribbled a note to Jade, warning her not to go out on her own, and saying he'd be back about lunchtime. He taped the note to the outside of the fridge door; Jade's first port of call in the morning was invariably the chilled concoction of orange juice and green tea she kept inside. Then he grabbed his phone and headed straight for the car.

He sped down the coast road to Hunmanby. His plan – seek Williams's help to find his mysterious stage partner, then enlist the small Egyptian spiritual worker in the search for Molly's killer.

If the police were right, then whoever had killed Molly

had also attacked Sandra and left her for dead. The reasons for this madness were unknown, but these were thoughts for another day. Today was about finding clues to the killer's identity using all the spiritual help he could muster. If the police got to the killer first, that was fine with Turner, but he was determined to do what he could, and do it quickly.

Concentrating hard on his driving, he ignored the beautiful coastal scenery dashing past. The clouds puffed and rushed by in an auburn glow and, out to sea, the rippling water looked like the rising sun had touched it and set it on fire. Lights flicked on in the houses as their sleepy tenants stretched and reached for the kettle. Curtains opened onto the dawn, laying out another day of work before the bliss of the weekend. The constant routine of work–sleep–work that drove many to boredom and a life of quiet desperation. Seagulls squawked and dive-bombed across the open fields, picking up scraps from the farmers' troughs before scavenging from the more lucrative tourists littering the beaches later in the day – tourists waiting for something to fulfil their fantasies before heading back to their own mundane routines.

Turner pulled into the caravan park and drove too fast over the speed bumps; his head banged painfully on the roof of the car. He didn't care – he needed help before anyone else was put in danger's way. He crunched up the gravel drive, hopped out of the car and hammered loudly on the front door of Williams's caravan.

Williams was already dressed in a sharp Italian suit with narrow lapels, and a pair of black penny loafers. He opened the door, ready to shoo away the unexpected visitor, but stopped short on seeing Turner.

'Bloody hell, you look terrible,' he said, scanning Turner's wrinkled shirt and unshaved chin. Dark circles under the visitor's eyes gave him a gaunt, desperate appearance. 'Come in, come in. But you'll have to wait in here. I'm doing a reading at the moment.'

Turner just had time to smile at the seated client before being pushed into a small room with two single beds next to the kitchen. Williams's client was a well-dressed woman in her late forties, and he noticed her clutching a handkerchief in her hand as if she'd been crying. Scattered on one of the beds was a series of postcards. With nothing else to do, Turner picked one up and read it.

Mrs Kelly Summers
X – Husband, Mike, heart attack, early forties
O – Callum, 7, football, Leeds United. 7th January
∞ – Christine, 12, likes horses. 19th September
 # – Money worries, new job (secretary)

Sitting 1
Recently bereaved. Doesn't like new job. Needs direction.

Sitting 2
Money tight. Lonely. Looking for companionship. No social life.

Recognising the coded symbols, Turner dropped the card onto the bed as if it were a live scorpion. Seeing a vision of his own past nauseated him. The cross on the postcard meant deceased, the circle a male child, the infinity symbol a female child, and the hash tag interests or concerns. It was a so-called 'poetry' card that fake mediums used to pass coded information between themselves about clients they'd worked with. A similar device existed in America called the 'Blue Book'. The passing of information between a tight network of fake spiritual workers made it a simple task for a skilled scammer to perform a miraculous reading for a client they'd never met – providing, of course, the client had already commissioned a reading from someone else in the network. The dates after the siblings' names were the birthdays. Turner knew all too well how the information on the card would be used in a sitting. The fake reader would say something like, 'I feel September is important to you. Somewhere in the middle of the month. Yes, I'm getting a date – September 19th. Does that mean anything to you?' After the usually shocked reply of 'Yes, it's my daughter's birthday', the standard follow-up would be, 'Well, your husband's just told me the date and wants you to know that he'll be there to celebrate it with you. He wants me to tell you he'll always be there for you. His love for you will never die.' Turner had done exactly the same thing himself many times back in the bad old days. But he'd never been stupid enough to write the 'poems' on cards. Even if he had, he would never have left them in plain sight. His preferred method had been via text, using emojis as the codes. That way, a casual glance at his phone as he pretended to turn it off before a reading would provide all he needed to know.

Remembering this made his nausea worse and he hunted around for a bottle of water, anything to cleanse himself of the guilt that twisted inside. Finding nothing, he shook his head and glanced for the fourth time at his watch. Looking for a distraction, he listened through the thin walls of the caravan to hear Williams continue his reading for his hapless client.

'Sorry about that. It's a friend of mine – he's arrived earlier than I expected,' Williams said, his voice pleasant and reassuring.

Turner leant closer to the wall to listen, amazed by the man's ability to deceive and disguise his true feelings. A jingling, as if something metallic was being picked up, echoed through the thin wall.

In the lounge, Williams cradled a pair of ebony-centred gold cufflinks in his palm. Closing his eyes briefly, he breathed in slowly before exhaling in a long sigh. An aromatherapy candle on the table swathed the room in a pleasant scent that calmed the mind and hinted at a church-like atmosphere.

He gazed over at his client. 'Yes, I can feel his presence. Your husband is standing behind you, just over your right shoulder.'

The woman turned but could see nothing.

Williams continued, his voice low and calm. 'He's telling me there's something unsaid. Something you wanted to tell him before he passed. Not a secret exactly, but something that's very important to you. Does that make sense to you?'

She nodded, wiping the tears trailing down her cheek.

Smiling and reaching out with his free hand to gently hold hers, Williams said, 'He tells me it's okay. You can tell him now. Please – he's right here.'

Trying to regain control, the woman pulled herself

upright on the foam settee and said, 'I'm sorry. Tell him I'm sorry for not being there when he passed.'

Williams squeezed her hand. 'I don't need to tell him – he can hear you. He's smiling at me and says I have to tell you not to worry. You were there for him when it mattered and he will always love you. He wants you to know he'll always be with you. That the love you shared will last for an eternity.' Smiling across the table, Williams passed back the cufflinks. 'He says you should carry these with you always. They'll bring you luck in everything you do.'

The woman placed the cufflinks in her purse. A weight seemed to have been lifted from her shoulders. She stood and moved to hug Williams. 'Thank you. Thank you so much. I can't tell you how much this means to me.'

Gratefully accepting the fifty pounds she offered, Williams said, 'I'm just pleased to have made contact for you. May God's love go with you.' And with that, he passed her a folded astrology chart and offered her a fond farewell, then watched her walk back to her caravan on the other side of the park still bathed in the sepia glow of the dawn.

A different Williams opened the door to the bedroom and glared at Turner. The smooth mask of deception had been dropped. 'What the hell are you doing here? You nearly bloody ruined that for me.' He stood, hands on hips, looking like an angry teapot in a suit.

For Turner, the contrast between what he'd heard through the walls of the caravan and his own experience with the ethereal spirit of Molly Craggs could not have been more marked. He'd listened to a sharp-dressed man pretend to see someone without demonstrating any proof that they were there. Then he'd heard a made-up conversation with the invisible visitor, and the sound of money changing hands for the bogus experience.

Turner knew that the ghostly figure of Molly Craggs he'd seen was real, or at least it had been to him – there'd been no one else in the room to tell him whether the spirit had truly manifested or he'd seen it in his head. But if his encounter was only a vision in his mind, then what difference was there between him and Williams? How would an unwitting member of the public know who to trust? A sickness grew inside him as he realised the answer – nobody could tell the difference. Listening to Williams was yet another reminder of exactly what and who he'd been.

The knowledge depressed him, and the best he could offer was, 'Sorry, I need your help.'

The clairvoyant had never seen Turner like this. He looked downtrodden, broken even. Ushering him into the lounge, he offered him a drink of water and urged him to sit down.

Turner explained about the murder of Molly Craggs and the alleged attack on Sandra Vaughan, skipping the gory details the police had told him, as it was still privileged information. He also left out any mention of the mysterious figure in the black dress that he'd seen after contacting the spirit of Molly Craggs, thinking that Williams wouldn't take him seriously. Finally, he suggested that the clairvoyant's Egyptian stage partner might have some spiritual insight into what was happening, given that she'd warned Jade about some impending danger at the show.

Williams scratched his head. He'd only met Sandra

Vaughan briefly, but that was nigh on four years ago, and he'd never met Molly Craggs. Yes, it was sad, tragic even, hearing about the murder and Sandra's battle for life, but he knew he had a busy schedule ahead of him and he needed Turner out of the way.

After a brief pause as he struggled with how to respond in the most empathetic way possible, he said, 'I'm sorry to hear about what's happened, but like I've already told you, I've only met the lady that does the Egyptian act a couple of times. I don't know where she lives or where she'll be now. We're not working together again until next week.'

Fidgeting with the tarot cards littering the table, he glanced up at the clock above the gas fire. He was expecting his next client in ten minutes and needed to get rid of his scruffy and funky-smelling visitor as quickly as possible. The sulphurous stink from the boiling hair still clung to Turner and Williams wrinkled his nose in self-defence as he moved closer.

'Let me try and find out where she is. But she's in the same game we are – anything she tells you will be made up if she thinks there's a profit in it. I wouldn't bother trying to find her if I was you. She seems a little crazy to me.'

He motioned Turner towards the front door as if he were shepherding a lost sheep. 'I'll do what I can, okay? But I'm not promising anything.'

Sliding behind the wheel, Turner felt more depressed than ever. He began turning things over in his mind. According to Williams, his Egyptian stage partner was a scammer as well. But if that were true, how come she'd given the warning to Jade? It wasn't something that formed part of the normal positive messages of love and comfort trooped out during such shows. It was as if Williams were trying to put him off contacting her. But why he'd want to do that, Turner had no idea.

Turner had felt something – fear – when the princess appeared on stage. His instincts had never let him down before. Perhaps of more concern was Williams describing himself as in the same game as Turner.

Feeling like he'd been bitten by a grief vampire and become infected, Turner wanted to cleanse himself, wash away the corruption that clung to him simply by being in the man's presence. Still driving too fast, his head crashed again on the roof of the car as he bounded over a speed bump.

This day was going from bad to worse, he thought, as he switched on the stereo and drove home, no further forward in his search for answers.

CHAPTER 15 – TERROR IN THE STREETS

Back in Whitby, Jade woke to find Turner's side of the bed cold and empty. The fact that he hadn't come to bed didn't surprise her. After she'd asked him not to stay up all night worrying, she'd already figured out that it would be an impossible task for him. Turner was always like that if he had things on his mind – he'd gnaw at the problem like a dog with a bone until he found answers.

Expecting to find him asleep or pacing the floor in the lounge, Jade stepped out of bed and straight onto a pile of rocks in a scrappy carrier bag. Yelping with pain, she crashed down, frantically rubbing her foot and cursing. Unfamiliar with the layout of Lee and Sandra's bedroom, she took a cautious look around to make sure there were no other booby traps ready to threaten her unwary digits.

Next to the bed, on top of a plain bedside cabinet, lay something that broke her heart. Sitting in a cheap frame was a photograph of Lee and Sandra travelling in Australia. Both wore huge cowboy hats as they grinned at the camera, the pair obviously delighted with their sunny adventure. Looking at Sandra's happy face brought back all the memories of her friend and the many thrilling experiences they'd shared. She caught her breath, trying to force down the tears that were welling inside her.

Dwelling in the bedroom was just too painful – she was immersed in all the familiar things that formed Sandra's life and loves. Needing a swift change of scenery, she bolted from the room, still limping, and set about hunting for her missing husband. Sadness clung to her, gripping her soul as she trotted across the corridor and pushed open the door to the lounge.

A strange smell wafted from the fireplace and she crinkled her nose as she explored further. In the corner of the cold embers, a cup was wedged bizarrely and appeared to contain a wisp of fine cotton or hair. Unwilling to brave the growing stench, she shook her head and wondered what on earth her husband had been up to.

Turner regularly did things like this, and many times she'd found the lounge table littered with strange texts, thick candles and odd ancient-looking objects. Asking him to explain produced either a non-committal response or a long, enthusiastic lecture on some nugget of lost knowledge he believed he'd discovered.

In truth, Turner's little 'experiments' with his supernatural gift fascinated her and she assumed the stinking cup was part of some bizarre ritual he'd thought up. Why, or for what purpose, she had no idea, but she hoped that Turner had found some spiritual insight into the horrific events of the past few days.

She was about to head down to the kitchen to quiz him about it when the door burst open and Kyle bounded in. If a dog's expression could say it had been crossing its legs for half an hour, then that was the one she was faced with now. Realising she needed to take him out for his morning constitutional or face a messy accident, Jade dressed and looked for his lead. As an afterthought, she grabbed the carrier bag full of rocks from the bedroom, thinking it would be easy to drop them off at Jurassic Jack's shop on the way up to the beach, and it would provide an excuse for her to break the news to him about Sandra. As far as she knew, Sandra's name was still being withheld from the media and it was likely that Jack had not connected the publicised discovery of a person found washed ashore with his fossil-hunting colleague.

Kyle pulled her through the kitchen like he was captain of a dog-sled team, and she missed the warning note Turner had left on the fridge.

Out in the cool morning air, she shivered as a salty breeze whistled down the road and prickled her face. Self-consciously, she pulled her thin top tight around her, regretting her decision to leave her coat behind. The car was missing from its regular parking spot, meaning that wherever Turner was, he was out and on the road already. Typical. He was probably chasing some idea or other on an impulse. If she were honest, though, she found his unpredictable nature exciting. One thing was for sure – life with Nathen Turner was never boring.

Sniffing the air in delight, the hairy hound yanked her onwards, bounding forward in great strides, loving the freedom after the confines of the house. It took all her strength to divert the pooch from his normal route as she guided him to the left and into the narrow, cobbled lane leading to Jurassic Jack's store.

She passed Kenny Florian, who was already out and wiping down the windows of The Alchemist, managing only a brief hello as her canine-propelled feet raced forward.

Kenny laughed, waved, and resumed his cleaning task, muttering, 'Bloody seagulls. Should all be shot,' as more of the sticky goo came off on his cloth.

The front door to the fossil-hunting emporium was ajar but Jade still knocked hesitantly on the glass panel as it was well before opening hours.

A rugged face walked forward from the back of the shop, growling and ready to shoo away the unwanted shopper. When Jack saw it was the familiar shape of Jade he beckoned her in and clipped Kyle's lead to a metal ring outside. Long experience had taught him that animals and his fossils, arranged on neat, well-organised glass shelves, didn't mix.

As he flicked on the lights, a vast array of shimmering stones and colourful crystals shone into life like he'd opened a glittering window into a prehistoric wonderland. The interior had a musty smell of earth and rock dust, but the overpowering scent came from Jack. Ever a man stuck in the past, he swore by Brut aftershave and certainly had not held back that morning. As a long-time boxing fan, Jack had settled on the cologne after Henry Cooper, that most famous of British fighters, had advertised it on television. If it was good enough for 'our 'enry' it was certainly good enough for him, he'd reasoned. Spicy notes mixed with the musk of the stones, creating a smell akin to the inside of a men's changing room after a sporting event.

Trying to breathe in as little of the heady bouquet as

possible, Jade handed over the bag of stones as Jack sat down behind the counter and tipped them out noisily on the top. 'These are from Sandra,' she said, not sure how to approach the real reason she'd called in.

Engrossed in the stones, Jack seemed not to have heard her. His mineral quarry was the love of his life and he turned the stones delicately in his calloused hands as if inspecting fine gemstones.

'Excellent. Yes, very good indeed. She's getting better. Look at this one.' His beaming face turned to Jade. She stared back blankly. Misinterpreting her expression as an acute lack of interest, he pushed the rock closer so she could examine it. Then he sensed that something was wrong. Not the smoothest with the ladies, he asked her outright. Her reaction was unexpected. Jade burst into tears. As long as he lived he'd never understand women, Jack thought, and wondered what on earth he should do now. Thankfully, she started talking before he had time to decide.

'Sandra's been injured. It's bad, Jack, really bad. They don't expect her to live. The person washed up on the beach, the one they talked about on the news, it was her.'

Jack slumped back in his chair, remembering the local news report from the previous evening. At the time, he'd thought it tragic, but then again it wasn't the first fossil hunter he'd heard about who'd met misfortune scavenging on the tidal shoreline. The sense of danger in his chosen profession was one of the things he liked; it made him feel more alive and grateful for each day. Now connecting the story with someone he knew, his previous detachment turned to pain. Without a personal connection to a place or person, stories of senseless violence, famines, floods and all the other things that formed part of the daily bulletin of human misery washed over him, as if he were watching a sad movie.

Still unsure of how best to handle his crying visitor, Jack stood and hugged Jade, his frame towering over her as if he cradled a distressed child. But she pulled away.

It wasn't that Jade hadn't appreciated the gesture; it was the smell of the aftershave up close and personal that threatened to smother her like an aromatic pillow.

Sucking in air, she stood still for a moment, trying to pull herself together.

From the street outside, a strange whining noise drifted into the shop and bounced around the cramped interior. Rising to a guttural howl, the sound filled her mind and clouded her senses. With head pounding, she rushed to the door to check on the dog.

Sitting peacefully outside, Kyle glanced up with drooping eyes and an expression on his furry face that clearly showed disappointment over the rude interruption to his morning walk.

But he wasn't howling.

The cobbled street seemed to amplify the noise, which screamed off the worn stones as if they were a bizarre echo chamber. She poked her head back inside the shop. 'Can you hear that, Jack? Like a howl – sounds terrifying.'

Shuffling from foot to foot, Jack looked at his visitor like she'd grown an extra head. Things were becoming way too weird for him. He was excellent at controlling his emotions and was internally processing the news about Sandra in as stoic a fashion as he could muster. Dealing with a crying woman hearing things was, however, in a different league.

'It's probably the barghest,' he said without thinking, and then regretted it.

According to local Whitby legend, the barghest was a huge black dog, eyes as bright as fire, that roamed the narrow streets at night. The beast was linked with demonic forces, and, if the stories were to be believed, only those about to die could hear its horrifying howl. Correcting himself quickly, he said, 'The barges. It's the barges – they're clearing out the harbour again. Maybe they're sounding their horns to warn other ships. Some of those horns do sound weird if you're not used to them.'

If they were sounding their horns, he couldn't hear them, but he kept that piece of information to himself. At the back of the shop, a glittering piece of Troller's Gill fluorite caught his gaze. Underneath the cluster of pale cubic crystals, tinged with purple at their edges, a large sign illustrated the mysterious dog and explained the barghest legend in vivid detail.

The limestone gorge of Troller's Gill in the Yorkshire Dales was another famed home of the phantom. Jack moved to stand in front of the sign, blocking it from Jade in case she'd heard him the first time. After a fossil-hunting trip to this lonely spot, Jack had proudly found some excellent crystals near the site of the old fluorspar mine and had thought that adding the bit about the barghest would improve their sales potential.

Jade, though, hadn't picked up on his comment and accepted the barge explanation with a slight shrug of her shoulders as the noise dwindled in her head.

After an uncomfortable exchange, where she'd asked Jack to spread the sad news to the owners of the bar where Sandra worked part time, she unfastened the depressed pooch and headed up the street.

In truth, Jack was glad to see her go. His inability to deal with Jade's emotional outburst had stretched him to his limit. Later, he'd process the news about Sandra in his own private way, but for now he had a shop to open. Putting on his happy face, he smiled at a couple of tourists passing by and flung open the door.

Relieved to be free again, Kyle sprinted up the cobblestone street, crossed the road and fled past the shops, eager to get to the beach.

Lost in her own thoughts, Jade trailed behind, not worried about the errant hound. Everybody knew him around here and it was doubtful he could get himself into much trouble. It was more likely he'd pick up a couple of dog treats from some of the locals on his travels.

She looked ahead and tasted the salt air, allowing it to cleanse her of the shop's musk.

Crowds milled down the narrow street, and the sun bathed the store windows and highlighted the enticing trinkets on display. Looking across to the harbour, Jade could see no sign of the barges she believed had made the weird howling she'd heard earlier. A teen on a skateboard weaved precariously through the throng, displaying fancy footwork as his gleaming sneakers expertly tilted to steer his route ahead. Guessing that the shoes cost more than her entire outfit, Jade wondered how modern parents afforded their children's obsession with the latest cool, and always expensive, fashion trends. The teenager provided a much-needed distraction, calming her mind and bringing her back to the everyday mediocrity of life.

The skateboarder whizzed past an old lady as she hobbled along, head down as if watching every step she took. The woman appeared to be struggling with the unevenness of the cobbles as she leant forward, stooped over her walking stick, giving her body a slight hunchback appearance. It was such a sad sight and Jade felt sorry for her – she seemed to be in pain and paused occasionally as if to get her breath back.

What she wore pulled in a few astonished looks from passers-by. Clothed head to foot in a loose black dress that stretched from her ankles to her wrists, she looked more Victorian than twenty-first century. Tap, tap, tap went the cane as it probed ahead for more secure footing, like a blind man's staff. Then the cane wedged between two loose stones and the woman fell to the ground with a yelp. Instinctively, Jade dashed to her side. She placed her arms gently underneath the prone torso and offered to support the old lady as she got to her feet.

'Thank you, dear,' a lisping voice said from underneath a tartan scarf wrapped across the women's mouth.

Bless her, thought Jade. She must be feeling the cold even though the sun streamed down, toasting the pavement. The eyes looking back at her seemed puffed, with heavy folds of skin under the lids, and the tangled grey hair didn't look natural – more like a cheap wig from the market.

Pulling her upright, Jade said, 'I'm happy to help. Are you okay? Where are you heading? Maybe I should walk with you to make sure you're all right.'

Limping even more now, the old woman accepted the help and led Jade down a narrow alley. A hatchback with its rear door open stood parked at the bottom.

'There's my car,' she said, pointing ahead. 'Silly me. I've left the door open again. I'm always doing that. Aren't we lucky we live in such a safe town?' Her voice was muffled by the scarf but clear enough for Jade to understand.

Jade nodded, not sure that Whitby was safe enough to leave a parked car with its door wide open. That, she thought, would be way too tempting for some of the characters she'd met.

The woman fished inside a hidden pocket in her dress for the key and opened the driver's door. She leant in and grabbed something from the passenger seat.

'Here, dear. Please accept this for your trouble.'

Things moved in a blur. A rag was violently pushed into Jade's mouth, stifling her cries for help, as her frail companion took on a new lease of life and bundled her into the back of the car. The rag had a sweet chemical smell and burned her lips. As she lay awkwardly on the back seat, Jade saw the woman reach up and remove the scarf from her face.

Through blurring vision, Jade watched the uncovered features move towards her and she tried to scream. Just before she lost consciousness she thought she heard the women say, 'Tell me, dear, do you think I'm pretty?'

CHAPTER 16 - THE HUNT IS ON

After searching the house on his return from Hunmanby and only finding a sleeping Lee, Turner stared at the note still fixed to the fridge door, warning Jade not to go out alone.

Woken by Turner, Lee now sat with his head in his hands at the foot of the stairs, exhausted after tossing and turning all right, unable to switch off the pain that clouded his thoughts.

A feeling of panic rose in Turner and he couldn't explain why. Things simply didn't feel right; he could sense it, but he hadn't the first idea what to do about it.

A polite tapping on the front door made Turner dash across the kitchen like an Olympic sprinter in a door-opening contest. Desperately hoping it was Jade and that she'd forgotten her key, what he saw made him stop short. Jack Reynolds, clad in his usual khaki ensemble, stood cradling a huge bunch of roses as he grinned at the fraught house owner.

Jack wasn't so much out of his depth with women as lost at sea – he needed water wings and a lifeguard standing by to cope with most of his encounters of the female kind. He'd been trying to figure out the right response after Jade had paid her tear-jerking visit to his shop that morning. After closing up earlier, he'd headed over the road to the pub where Sandra worked to break the news to its owners, before a quick trip to the florist. He didn't know Jade that well, so, as most men did when out of their emotional depth, he'd bought flowers.

Turner gazed in wonder at this leather-faced outdoorsman standing awkwardly on his doorstep with a dainty bouquet.

Blushing and looking distinctly uncomfortable, Jack said, 'I've brought these for Jade. She was in earlier to tell me about Sandra—'

Within seconds, Turner had Jack seated, and started firing questions. This direct, if brutal, style of conversation was much easier for the fossil-hunting alpha male to cope with. Straight-talking he could handle; it was the emotional Russian roulette of his brushes with the female of the species that confused him. Finding that Jade hadn't returned to the house, Jack's words tumbled out as he told Turner all he could remember about her visit to his shop.

Fidgeting with a delicate petal, he said, 'She was in a pretty bad way. Upset, I mean. Then she started hearing things.'

The flowers seemed to be taking all of Jack's attention and he refused to meet anyone's gaze.

Having spent a lifetime reading people for a living, Turner could see guilt and remorse written all over his visitor's face. In no mood to pussyfoot around the edges, he said, 'What did you do, Jack? You did something, didn't you?'

He took a step closer to the table.

Now a leaf seemed to be the most interesting thing in the world as Jack stroked it between his finger and thumb.

'Tell me what you did!'

Turner grabbed the flowers and threw them in the sink as his frustration got the better of him.

Without the posy to distract him, Jack looked up to the exasperated face towering above him. 'Well, she said she could hear a shrieking howl that scared her. I mean ... there wasn't anything – no noise at all. So ... I just made a joke, that's all.' He glanced at the crumpled petals in the sink, longing to have something to occupy his fidgeting fingers. 'I said the noise was the barghest. But she didn't hear me; at least, I don't think she did.'

Watching his pacing host apprehensively, the fossil hunter hoped Turner would see the funny side.

He didn't. The legendary phantom dog had featured in many tales from Turner's past life and it was a popular story on many of his ghost-hunting tours. He, more than anybody, knew the significance of hearing the hound's deathly dirge. It meant his wife was about to die. He recalled the night of the clairvoyant show – he'd thought he'd seen a large black dog following Molly's car. Now she was dead and his wife was out somewhere, alone. Icy fingers seemed to claw Turner's spine as his growing panic was replaced by fear.

Oblivious to the inner feelings of his host, Jack sat buttoning and unbuttoning his shirt cuff.

Turner grabbed his wrist to stop him; his hand looked like a child's next to the calloused mitt.

Jack had gone pink again and rushed out his cover story of the barges in the harbour.

Turner crouched down so he was at eye level with the seated adventurer and said, 'And you didn't hear any of these sounds yourself?'

'No.' The pink was now a glowing red – Jack's skin appeared to be incinerating from the inside out.

'Right, that settles it. Lee, grab your coat. We're going out to find her.'

He ushered Jack to his feet and out the door, then tugged Lee by the arm and catapulted him into the street.

As Lee regained his balance, a hairy hound came bounding up and flattened him. Stinky breath steamed across his face as a rough tongue licked wetly at his cheek.

Lee laughed at Kyle's familiar greeting. He'd never been so happy to see the errant pooch in his life, and flung his arms around him, wrestling with him on the floor. Finally, covered in dust and grime from the pavement, he stood and said, 'Ta-dah.'

Turner was busy locking the door. As he spun to face Lee, he was pounced on and pushed back hard against the door, all the wind knocked out of him. Feeling the shaggy paws and mountain of hair ramming against his legs, his immediate thought was that the barghest had come for him. Realising it was Kyle, he sunk to his knees, kissed the dog on the head and cradled its huge face in his arms. Then he looked along the street, expecting to find Jade.

'Where is she, boy?' Turner said, expecting the dog to understand him.

Trying to push past Turner and get a much-needed drink and snack from the kitchen, the hungry mutt ignored the question, his eyes imploring his owner to let him inside.

After wandering the streets for hours, trying to find Jade, all that filled the furry head was the drive for food and water. His doggy brain had just assumed Jade had gone home without him.

After a brief trip inside to cram half a tin of dog food down the hungry hound, the trio set off, combing the streets for Jade. Turner let Kyle take the front. 'Find her, boy. Find her.'

With nose pressed to the cobbles, the dog sniffed and snorted his way forward, stopping occasionally to smell the air. The lead was pulled taut in Turner's hand as Kyle pressed on, retracing his route up to the beach. He was enjoying this game and his tail wagged furiously behind him.

'Looks like he's on a mission,' a familiar voice called out from one of the shops lining the narrow street. The figure pointed down and smiled at the straining dog.

Turner glanced across to see the slim profile of Beccy McCall, co-owner of the local fishmonger's. She stood, hands on hips, ready to shut up the shop, still dressed in her striped red apron. Pulling off her blue hair net, she walked over and stroked the dog. 'Twice in one day, eh? Aren't you the lucky boy?' Playfully, she tickled under Kyle's hairy chin.

Willing to grasp at any straw that would help him find his wife, Turner began bombarding her with questions.

Taken aback by the torrent of words flooding from the psychic, whose eyes were darting up and down the street as if looking for something, Beccy put her hand on his shoulder and said, 'You okay? What's wrong? Why the interrogation? You haven't even said hello yet.'

Realising that his anxiety had got the better of him,

Turner muttered an apology. Lee shuffled his feet, idly scuffing his soles against the stones, embarrassed at his friend's blunt manner with the fishmonger. They'd known Beccy and her husband for as long as he could remember and as well as being a past client of Turner's, she was also purveyor of the freshest fish in the town.

She leant back against the shop window. All that was left on display were a couple of open shark jaws, their sharp teeth glistening in the fading sun; the fresh produce had been returned to the freezers at the back. The monster jaws in the window were great for bringing tourists into the shop to ask if sharks were found locally, and whether it was safe to swim in the bay. It always made her laugh, and invariably, after a brief reassurance, the tourists would pick up some tasty crab or other titbit to snack on.

Explaining that Jade hadn't returned home, Turner asked, more politely this time, whether Beccy had seen her walking the dog earlier.

Beccy pointed up the street. 'Yes, they passed by this morning. Last time I saw Jade she was helping some old dear over there. Poor thing.'

Turner raised his eyebrows before realising she'd referred to the old woman and not Jade. 'It looked like she'd been to a funeral. All dressed in black she was – head to toe. I think she lost her footing and fell over. Not surprising when you saw how heavily she leant on that cane of hers.' Beccy sighed and shook her head. 'Age, eh? Comes to us all. Reminds me of old Sandy. Remember him ...'

Before she could launch into a long monologue about the perils of old Sandy, Turner made his excuses to leave.

Beccy was a lovely woman but when the mood was upon her she could talk the hind leg off a very large donkey. He didn't have time for that, today of all days.

They left her there, still talking to no one in particular about the time old Sandy had fallen and been taken to hospital, and pushed ahead up the street, steered by the dog.

Turner picked up the pace. The description of the old woman was exactly the same as the figure he'd seen in his vision – if he could call it that – during his time with the departed spirit of Molly Craggs. Molly had answered the door to somebody dressed like that, or at least that's what he'd thought he'd seen. Plus, this was way too close to the dream that had woken him in a cold sweat where a similar figure had carried Jade's severed head in a wicker basket. Trying to explain these supernatural experiences to Lee would be impossible, so he kept quiet and followed the dog. With palms sweating and a growing feeling of unease, Turner pushed on, glancing into every corner for any signs of his wife.

At the top of an alley, Kyle veered left and bounded forward. Hanging on for grim death, the pair followed behind as the dog pushed on, straining at the leash. At the end of the narrow pathway that cut between the houses, Kyle stopped and looked around, all traces of the scent trail lost. They'd come out on a cramped street that served as an access road and prime parking spot for the locals. Looking up and down, they saw one or two empty cars parked carelessly, their wheels halfway over the pavement.

Turner looked across the bay to the huge whalebone arch that sat on top of the West Cliff. The sun was beginning to set behind it, bathing the sea in an orange glow as it foamed across the sands. Underneath, on the harbour road, the sound of the amusement arcades chimed and chirped as he watched a gang of teens shuffling change in their hands before heading inside. Normal, everyday life in Whitby, settling into the evening ahead. But his life was far from normal at the moment. Amid this ordinary scene, he gazed at the horizon and considered his next move.

His mobile rang. 'Jade, is that you?' he said, holding his breath as he waited for an answer.

The response surprised him.

Laughter.

After the chuckling stopped, Williams said, 'Still don't recognise me after all these years, eh? Anyway, I haven't got the legs to be your missus.'

Turner was not enjoying the joke and said so.

'Don't be like that – I'm only kidding with you. You were looking for that creepy Egyptian act, Princess Amunet. Well, I've found her. But I still think you're better off leaving her well alone. I think she's a little nuts.'

Over a short, and terse call, Williams passed on the information at Turner's insistence. The following day, Princess Amunet had a stall booked at a psychic fair hosted by a school over in Scarborough.

Scribbling down the details in a red notebook he kept in his jeans pocket, Turner thanked him and apologised for his manner. It seemed like he was spending a lot of time asking for forgiveness today.

Gazing back out to sea, the fear inside him grew like an all-consuming cancer, and it tore him apart. He felt certain that the figure described so eloquently by the amiable fishmonger was the same one who'd called on Molly Craggs shortly before her death.

He needed help – not the police; this was beyond their earthly confines. The assistance he needed didn't belong to this world; it belonged to the supernatural – a realm he felt comfortable in and that had saved his life more than once. But he knew he couldn't do it on his own. Up to now he'd used his skills to channel departed spirits, or they'd contacted him for help. Occasionally, he'd see things in his dreams that guided his decisions and put him on the right path to solving a mystery or helping others. But he'd never been good at seeing future events or divining information about those in the mortal plane. His realm was the dead.

He needed someone who had the skills he lacked. Princess Amunet had warned Jade about the danger, and she'd been right. Perhaps she had this gift of divining the future, and maybe, with her help, he could get some clues to what had happened to his wife.

He hoped so. If he was wrong about the princess and she was simply another scammer, there would be little hope of a happy ending in his mind.

He needed desperately to find out what else the princess knew, and he needed to do it quickly.

CHAPTER 17 – THE PSYCHIC FAIR

After combing the streets well into the evening gloom, Turner returned home exhausted. But sleep wouldn't come. He sat idly stroking the dog, which lay dozing next to the fire in the lounge, as his mind spun cartwheels trying to figure out what else he could do.

Lee had telephoned the hospital and seemed in better spirits. Sandra was still fighting, hanging onto the thread of her life, and the medical team had said they were pleased with her progress. After trying to console his lifelong friend and reassure him that Jade would show up soon, an exhausted Lee had headed to bed.

Turner poured over an ancient text he'd removed from his library in the bedroom, hunting for a method for divining what had happened and where Jade was. This was the fourth text he'd tried from his collection of ancient manuscripts; none so far had been of any use.

Turning his mind to the Egyptian princess, he pulled over a book on ancient Egyptian spells and incantations. Maybe he could find something that he and the princess could use, channelling both their energies to maximise the effect, to make contact with the spirit of Molly Craggs again.

Flipping to a section attributed to a spell book used by Ramses III, he read through a section entitled 'Resurrection Spells – Coming Forth by Day'.

The text described the use of a human-shaped wax figure the length of an open hand and with a hollow in the back. After filling the hollow with an appropriate written spell and something belonging to the person to be resurrected, the figure was to be burnt in a fire. Maybe he could use this to bring back the spirit of Molly, but this time with a stronger connection.

After frantically flicking through more pages, he was disappointed to find no transcription or translation of any appropriate spell. Another dead end. His life seemed full of them at the moment.

With more questions than answers, he curled up on the settee and spent a restless night tossing and turning as his dreams turned to creepy figures clothed in black and the cold dead face of Molly Craggs.

The dog woke him by pawing at his leg. Without wasting any more time, Turner hastily passed custody of Kyle to Lee and set off to the psychic fair in search of Princess Amunet.

He'd forgotten to eat and his stomach grumbled loudly as he pulled into the visitors' car park of the school. But it wasn't just the lack of nourishment churning in his gut; he felt empty and alone without the love of his life. He'd never contemplated life without her, and the thought that she might be in danger, or already be dead, was too horrible for him to think about. He needed to stay focused on unravelling the mystery and keep such morbid ideas from his mind. With a small glimmer of hope in his heart, he locked the car and headed inside.

The red-brick facade of the school had seen better days and crumbling mortar lined the path up to the steps facing the large doorway. A polite woman in a baggy jumper smiled at him and took the small entrance fee before beckoning him inside with a smile. Large home-printed arrows pointed the way down a doglegged corridor that led to the school hall. Flaking magnolia paint surrounded cork boards filled with children's schoolwork and colourful illustrations. They'd certainly done their best to brighten up the place, despite the obvious need for a decorator's brush. The unmistakeable smell of bleach filled his nostrils after some over-enthusiastic cleaner had set about making the place as spick and span as possible for the fair. Burgundy carpet tiles cushioned his steps as he padded along.

He reached a couple of vinyl banners saying 'Welcome to the Psychic Fair. Your destiny awaits within' either side of the doorway into a large hall. He'd often wondered whether anybody bothered clearing the copyright for the myriad of professional images on the posters showing crystal balls, palm reading, tarot cards and the like. Unlikely, he thought, as he'd never done so himself, instead pulling off random images from the Internet that suited his style and business stationery back in his scamming days. He doubted whether copyright theft would bother any of the colourful characters he'd met at previous fairs across the country, and guessed they'd seek forgiveness rather than permission if they were ever challenged.

As he stepped in and took his first look around, the

peroxide smell of the corridor was replaced by a combination of sandalwood and jasmine from a couple of candles burning in the corner of the hall. It gave the space a calming and spiritual feel. Some fifteen to twenty tables stood in a horseshoe shape, their surfaces littered with colourful leaflets advertising herbal remedies, aromatherapy, Indian head massage and various exciting-sounding divination opportunities. Palm readers sat chatting with purveyors of feather dreamcatchers, discussing the finer points of their metaphysical experiences. Some diviners had gone the extra mile; beautiful roll-up banners advertising their services were propped proudly alongside their tables. The banners had a smiling professional headshot that made the diviner look like a movie star, with a few quotes underneath from past clients endorsing their services.

Glancing at the nearest tarot-card reader's stall, Turner could see that business was already booming. A clear-framed waitlist stood on the table, showing the names and times of readings, and it was already half full. Next to the tarot reader, a slim man in a smart suit sat behind a row of glittering pendants hanging from a wooden rack. Cut crystal and coloured gemstones dangled from an array of leather and hemp cords that swayed back and forth every time someone opened the hall door. Together, they looked like a kind of spiritual chandelier glinting in the light from the windows. A beige sign underneath read 'Custom pendants available. Handcrafted by a master artisan. We ship worldwide'.

The whole place had the look of an indoor car-boot sale for the spirit realm, and Turner adored it. He'd spent many happy hours in places like this, chatting with people about subjects that fascinated him. The fairs had also provided a great opportunity for him to stock up on tarot cards or enhance his already huge book collection. Yes, the atmosphere had a socialist, ban the bomb, hippy vibe, but it was calming and he needed to restore some sort of peace to his troubled mind.

Looking at the smiling faces around the room, he recognised about half of them from his past life as a fake psychic medium. He said a few quick and polite hellos as he walked to the back of the hall, hunting for Princess Amunet.

He found her stall tucked in a corner next to the stage at the far end of the room. In contrast with the other colourful exhibitors, all she had on display was an ancient-looking stone ankh, set centrally on a small table draped with some sort of hairy animal skin, stained black. She sat behind the table in a smart purple pantsuit with an emerald crocodile brooch gleaming on the lapel. The shoulder-length ebony braids and heavy eye makeup emphasised her smooth skin and almond eyes, which seemed to take in everything and nothing at the same time as she smiled at the passers-by. Not sure how to make his introduction, Turner hesitated, feeling the sheer presence of the woman. He'd sensed a connection with her he couldn't quite explain and it made him uncomfortable.

The princess looked up and gazed straight into his eyes, sizing up what this strange man in the loud Hawaiian shirt wanted as he rocked from toe to toe with his hands in his pockets.

'Hello again, Nathen Turner,' she said, still keeping eye contact. 'Please sit. There's much we have to talk about.'

The voice was soft and gentle, like a mother talking lovingly to a young child.

Turner did as he was told, his skin tingling as if he'd been plugged into an electric socket. 'Erm ... hello, Princess. How do you know my name?'

A giggle, like a teenage girl's, caused the princess to self-consciously cover her mouth. 'We've met before. You were at the show with your wife.'

True, he thought, but they'd never actually met. So far the signs were good; it definitely looked as if his Egyptian companion had some sort of spiritual gift. He nodded back, still not sure what to say.

The smile faded from the smooth features as the princess flicked back her hair and held his gaze. 'Your wife is missing and you want my help.' It was a statement not a question.

The direct eye contact made Turner wriggle in his seat – she never seemed to blink. He nodded again, feeling in awe of this petite woman. There was no way she could have known about Jade, and his confidence in her ability was growing. He could only wonder how she'd discovered her spiritual gift, but for now he pushed it to the back of his mind as he sank down in his chair to a more comfortable position.

The princess reached out, wrapped her hands around the stone ankh and closed her eyes. Thank God, thought Turner, pleased to be free of the almond stare. Her breathing slowed and he could see her chest rising and falling, causing the crocodile brooch to glint and fade in rhythm as it caught the light. Turner looked around, feeling self-conscious about sitting across from somebody who sat silently fondling an ancient relic. No one paid them any attention – they were all engrossed in their own particular spiritual fix. Relieved, he looked back at the seated figure. Nothing had changed, so he began to fidget again on the plastic chair, more designed for a child than a lanky psychic. His backside began to ache on the hard plastic torture seat. He rocked back and forward, relieving the pressure on his sore buttocks. At least it took his mind off his situation.

The princess's eyes flicked open and locked onto him. Turner felt a shiver down his spine and he sat bolt upright, expecting an outpouring of news on Jade's whereabouts. Instead, she reached underneath the table and took out a pack of tarot cards, the like of which he'd never seen. Emblazoned across the back, in stunning gold leaf on a deep-blue background, was a large crocodile whose design matched her brooch.

Pushing them across the table, she said, 'Please mix the cards.'

If he were doing a reading, at this stage he'd ask the sitter to concentrate on connecting their energy with the deck, or something similar. There was no such preamble here, just a simple instruction.

After cutting the pack in two, he grabbed the smaller edges of the large cards awkwardly between his outstretched thumbs and little fingers, and riffled the two halves. As the cards clicked noisily together, Turner felt the hairy tablecloth rubbing under the palms of his hands like he was shuffling on the back of a bear. The amber gaze was back, lasering through him as he clumsily pushed the shuffled deck back across the table.

Almost in slow motion, she spread the face-down

deck evenly from one side to the other.

'Please touch a card and pull it towards you,' the princess said, smiling in a way that Turner hoped was meant to give him reassurance. Again, there was no attempt at spiritual small talk, just direct instruction.

Looking across the golden backs, he pushed out his right hand and hovered over the spread. Not sure if he was imagining things, he felt his palm prickle as if it were drawing energy up into his body from the cards. Roughly in the centre, he allowed his forefinger to bend down and touch the back of a card before smoothly sliding it towards himself. There was a brief static shock to his forefinger that made him jump. He guessed, rightly, that the hairy material covering the table was meant to build up static in the sitter's hands as they shuffled, creating this unusual effect. None of that surprised him; he'd seen magicians use similar methods before, and he could only admire the princess's flair and showmanship. If this *was* an act, she was really, really good at it. Although the sceptic in him was taking a back seat, his psychic radar twitched for any signs of a scam.

Slowly, the princess allowed her breath to sigh from her lips as she reached over and flipped the card face up. Again, the design was unfamiliar to Turner. Over the years he'd studiously collected hundreds of tarot decks and thought he knew them all. This particular set looked custom-made by a skilled artist, and he marvelled at the artwork. Enclosed in a gilt border was the single figure of a man, mummified from head to toe, only his head and hands exposed, the uncovered skin shaded dark green. A cone-like headdress pointed up to the top border; a long plumed feather at each side gave the head covering a lopsided appearance. In his hands, the figure held a flail and a shepherd's crook. Turner's heart sank as recognition finally set in. It was a depiction of Osiris, the Egyptian god of the dead.

As if reading his thoughts, the princess said, 'Jade is alive.' Her face appeared devoid of any emotion. It was as if she felt no connection to the words, her smooth complexion untouched by the news she was about to give. 'But she's not safe. The card depicts the coming of a judgement of life or death from someone who means to harm her.'

Hearing that his wife wasn't dead, Turner slumped with relief. This time he locked his gaze onto the princess, putting aside how uncomfortable it felt. 'Can you tell me where she is?' He placed his elbows on the table and leant forward to make sure he heard everything clearly in the noisy room.

The unimpassioned face of the princess gazed back. Reaching over to cradle the stone ankh in her hands, she briefly closed her eyes and began to stroke her fingers gently over it, tracing the outline. Turner was now past caring what others might think of him sitting across from somebody caressing a stone in such a sensual manner. Biting his lip, he waited and watched, tapping his feet under the table.

After what seemed like an eternity, the princess opened her eyes. 'There's a woman in black. An evil person. She wants to hurt her.'

As she spoke, the words seemed slightly out of sync with her mouth, an effect he'd noticed at the stage show. Barely noticeable, but it was there. It gave her a strange, otherworldly quality, as if the words weren't her own, as if she were a conduit from a mystical plane.

'I see a large house, old in design. There's a weathervane on the roof in the shape of a griffin. It's a vicarage. No, it used to be. There are fields, many fields around it, and trees. Many trees. She's kept there.' She clasped her hands together as if praying, her cold features still unmoving. 'There's a large gravel drive. It's many miles from here. Inland, but I'm not sure how far. Yes, she's kept there. You must find her. I cannot tell you if you will be successful; that is for fate to decide.' Her posture relaxed and now the frigid features smiled across the table as if she'd given him a sure bet on the next horse race.

Turner tried to probe further, but the princess could offer nothing more and sat smiling coolly back at him. There was no reason to doubt what he'd been told; the mystical Egyptian seer could gain no benefit from her reading and he'd offered no money for her time. Frustrated, but grateful for the help, Turner thanked her.

As an afterthought, he said, 'How can I find you again? Do you have any contact details? Would you help me again if I needed it?'

For the first time the princess stood, her small frame dwarfed by the psychic. She reached out a hand and he shook it, feeling a dry coolness against his palm. Up close, he didn't detect any scent to speak of, which he found strange. All the women he knew prided themselves on their perfume collection, or at least had a favourite they religiously stuck to. If anything, her faint odour reminded him of a new car, and he dismissed it, thinking he was imagining things.

Staring straight at him, she said, 'You will find me if you need me. If it's our destiny to meet again, then we will.'

Thanking her again, Turner raced back to his car,

ignoring the greetings from past colleagues and clients as he headed out the door.

Later, he'd reflect on and process this surreal experience with the princess. But for now he had only one thing on his mind. Find his wife or die trying.

CHAPTER 18 – PAIN IN THE SHADOWS

The small figure held her knees in the cramped space and sobbed. Surrounding her was blackness, pure and total. The odd drip of water slapped down onto the concrete floor, making her jump in the silence. How long she'd been in this gloomy space she had no idea. The last thing she remembered was helping an old lady to her car before everything had faded. Then Jade Turner had woken up, chained and alone in this godforsaken pit. The manacles that secured her to the wall allowed her to explore only about two feet either side, but that was just far enough to touch the walls. She could feel mould crumbling under her fingers and the air smelled stale and dank. Despair flooded her mind. Calling for help had got no answer expect the drip, drip, drip of the water down the wall.

Occasionally, she thought she heard voices up above; a man and a woman seemed to be arguing furiously about something. The words were unclear but the emotions weren't. Thumping footsteps passed by to the left and right but never overhead.

Gazing into the blackness, she began to imagine shapes – weird monsters rising from the shadows, dripping fangs and sharp claws ready to rend her apart at any moment. Her position on the cold concrete gradually chilled her to the bone and she began to shiver uncontrollably. Wave after wave of tremors rattled her frame as she cradled her knees and rocked backwards and forwards. She thought of Nathen, Lee and Sandra, and their life together at the house. Looking for a favourite memory to warm her shivering soul, she settled on the first time she'd met Turner in Las Vegas. He'd been heading home on her flight and the two had shared a few laughs and a connection that had stayed with them ever since. Picturing his smiling face, she talked to him in her thoughts, calling out to him to find her. Save her. Rescue her from this sunken grave.

A loud scraping above her head made her duck instinctively; it sounded as if a heavy object were being slid out of the way. Then a small chink of light appeared that blinded her. It grew bigger, bit by slow bit. She reached out, shouting again for help, but her voice was met with laughter from above. A man's eyes peered through the gap. Behind him a woman said, 'Well, is that her?' The man said yes before closing the gap again and plunging her back into darkness.

Now the voices were muffled but Jade could make out the words more clearly. The man swore at the woman. From what she could hear he was vehemently chastising her about something. Then the scraping noise above her head was back and the voices faded away.

Exhaustion overcame her, and her head drooped to her chest. She dozed fitfully, waking at the slightest noise. How long she rested was impossible to tell in the inky blackness, her senses now blocked from any impression of time. Then the scraping overhead woke her up again and she began to cry. She felt helpless, and could see no glimmer of hope for the future, any future. She knew she was dead, or at least would be shortly. Why else would she have been brought here and treated like this? What possible reason could someone have? The questions rattled unanswered around her brain.

The light was back, searing her vision, making her flinch with pain as she tried to readjust to the brightness. Gradually the shimmering haze refocused and she could see the figure of an old woman in black gazing down. It must be the same lady she'd tried to help in the street, she thought, but the scarf around her mouth had been replaced with a black veil, making her look like some sort of ghoulish bride.

The light allowed her to see her confines properly for the first time. It was a concrete hole about six feet deep and four feet square. The old woman threw down a bottle of water that slapped the trembling captive on the thigh.

Kneeling down, the old woman said, 'Drink this, dear. We don't want you dying just yet.' Laughter cackled down into the hole.

Jade pulled at the top of the bottle, wrestling the cap with her bound hands. More laughter came from above. After a struggle, she managed to unscrew the lid and eagerly gulped down the water. It spilled onto her chin and soaked her blouse, but she didn't care.

'Why are you doing this to me? Why trap and bind me like this?'

There was a pause as the veiled face of the old woman leered into the hole. Slowly she heaved up the covering on the concrete prison and sat on the edge of the pit, her legs dangling down inches from Jade's face. For a while the dark figure seemed to be studying its prisoner like an exhibit in a zoo.

'You're very pretty, my dear. It's such a shame.' The emotion in the voice made it obvious that this woman felt no shame at all. There was an excitement in it, like someone nervously waiting for a much-anticipated surprise.

Watching the legs bounce back and forward off the wall as she spoke, Jade knew the woman was enjoying herself, relishing in the moment. Taking another sip to quench her parched throat, Jade looked up defiantly. 'I don't know who you are or what you're going to do with me but your silly dress and this whole charade doesn't scare me.'

In truth, it terrified her, but to admit as much to this psycho would only add to the woman's enjoyment. If she were going to die, then she wanted to make sure she made it as hard as possible for this obvious mental case.

Again, laughter – a cackle accompanied by more excited leg swinging that passed dangerously close to Jade's head. The buckles on the woman's shiny shoes glinted in and out of the light from above as her feet brushed Jade's cheek.

Fearing the woman might kick her in the face, Jade pulled away as far as her manacles would allow.

Seeing Jade scuttle across the concrete floor caused more chuckling from above. 'Not afraid, eh? Look at you, cowering in the corner,' the old woman said, leaning forward. 'You look like a frightened little girl to me, dear. And you should be.'

This was too much for Jade and she began to sob again, all pretence of defiance gone. Tears mingled with the concrete dust on her face and she rubbed them away furiously, trying to regain her composure. But she couldn't. She was beaten, helpless and at the complete mercy of this crazed woman who looked like Queen Victoria had mated with the devil.

Jade's arms began to shake and she dropped the bottle of water and hugged her knees to her again, rocking backwards and forwards on the hard floor.

The woman watched from behind her veil, feeling the rush of complete power over another human being. This was more fun than she'd imagined; the trembling girl below enthralled her. Watching her captive break and crumble into a quivering wreck was exciting. No, it was more than that. It was great fun.

Pulling hard at the manacles, Jade tried vainly to move, reaching up to grab at the woman's ankles. Maybe if she could pull the woman into the hole, then she'd have a chance to overcome the psychopath and find some way of escape. She clawed desperately at the empty air but couldn't reach. The woman stood and towered over her. A lamp behind silhouetted the dark figure, which remained still and silent, looking into the hole, tilting her head as if fascinated.

Between sobs, Jade looked up, squinting into the light. 'Why have you brought me here? What do you want from me?' Her body jerked awkwardly as if she were beginning to have a fit.

The sound of more laughter from above enveloped Jade, mocking her.

'You'll find out soon enough, dear. Be patient and enjoy the time you have left. We're waiting for your husband to find you and then you'll be free. Forever.'

The cackling faded as the concrete prison was sealed back up again into blackness.

Jade wailed into the dark, her sorrowful cries echoing off the walls and filling the small space. This was too horrible to imagine. For some reason a raving psychopath – no, she'd heard two of them – two complete and utter crazy people had trapped her with the single intention of getting to her husband. They'd already killed Molly Craggs and attacked Sandra Vaughan – it must be the same team. Now it looked like Jade and Nathen were the next victims they'd add to their collection.

Her work as an airline stewardess had trained her to be calm in times of crisis but this experience had broken her, shattered her terrified mind. Wailing inconsolably, cradling her knees and rocking back and forth, she prayed for one thing.

That her husband *wouldn't* find her.

CHAPTER 19 – SEARCHING ON THE MOORS

The silver VW Golf hared across the moorland roads as if a demon were on its tail. Inside, three men sat peering out the windows, looking for buildings that matched the description given by the princess at the fair.

Turner concentrated hard as he drove, leaning forward in his seat as if it would make the car go faster. Lee sat slouched in the passenger seat, still exhausted after the ordeal of the past couple of days. He was lost in his internal musings, couldn't put them into words and didn't feel comfortable talking to anyone about them.

Sandra was still alive, but for how long? And, if she did recover, what state would she be in? The doctors had told him there might be brain damage and/or paralysis if she did pull through, but had asked him to stay positive. That was easy for them to say, he thought. It wasn't their soul mate lying in a coma. All he knew was, he felt disorientated – wracked by the sea of emotions drowning him. And now Jade had gone missing. The whole thing was overwhelming, and he tried hard to fight off the fatigue that gripped him as he scanned the road ahead.

After leaving the psychic fair, Turner had phoned the

police to report Jade missing and pass on the clues to her possible location. A stern officer had asked him if she'd been missing for twenty-four hours. When the answer came back in the negative, the officer had regretted that there was nothing he could do at that stage and had asked Turner to call back if she hadn't come back by the evening. Exasperated, Turner had rung Lee and told him what he knew before asking him to get hold of his friend and drinking companion, Tony. He'd hoped that Tony was off-duty and would join them in an unofficial capacity to help with the search.

Neither Turner nor Lee were men of violence and would likely be unable to fight their way out of a wet paper bag. Tony, on the other hand, was an old-school copper. He'd risen through the ranks from a time when it had been acceptable to give the odd villain a more physical and unofficial retribution, rather than lock them up. That, of course, was unacceptable these days, and any such action was likely to lead to the wrongdoer suing the police in the current climate of human rights – one that many on the force felt had gone too far. Pussyfooting around a violent thug was always a recipe for disaster, but the police had little choice; they tried to be as civil as possible while being spat at and punched in the face. The no-win, no-fee legal vultures hadn't helped the cause either, bringing free legal aid to any scumbag who wanted to chance their arm and make a claim.

Turner needed Tony if things turned ugly, and the off-duty policeman now sat in the back of the car. He flicked out his ASP baton and tapped it gently on Turner's sleeping dog, who lay snoozing on his lap. Like Lee, Tony sported a plain T-shirt and jeans in contrast to Turner's loud shirt. The fabric on the policeman's shirt clung tightly over his muscled frame, making Lee look like a scrawny reject from a body-building contest. Not exactly *Reservoir Dogs*, but the trio, plus their furry companion, were still intent on dealing with whatever they'd face, and suffer any legal consequences later.

After being told by the princess that Jade was being held at an old vicarage inland, Turner had printed out several possible locations from the Internet. He'd settled his attention around the abbey and monastery sites that littered the North York moors. Many had an associated vicarage that had been converted to a domestic dwelling, so he'd felt this was as good a place as any to start. He desperately needed to do something. Sitting at home and twiddling his thumbs was simply not an option.

They'd already sped around Grosmont Priory, Handale Priory and Mount Grace Priory with no success before heading south towards Rosedale.

Rubbing vigorously at his face, Lee chanced a glance at Turner, who he could see was hurting inside. 'We'll find her. Don't worry. We always find a way of pulling through together, don't we?' He patted Turner reassuringly on the shoulder.

Turner rammed the accelerator, causing the car to leap forward and push them all back in their seats. Lee reached up and grabbed the strap above the window as the cabin rocked back and forth along the winding roads.

Shaking his head in an attempt to clear his depressing thoughts, Turner said, 'I hope so, Lee. I just feel so helpless, you know? It's like living through a nightmare.'

Lee reached up to the dashboard, grabbed a loose sheaf of maps printed from the Internet and began to scan them. 'So, we're looking for a place with a gravel drive, and with some fields and trees around it, yes?'

Turner nodded.

Thinking that this described every property in the area, the guitarist nevertheless spread out the sheets to see if he could find anything.

Turner concentrated on the road ahead. The purple heather moorland gave way to a verdant treelined valley as he made his way down the steep slopes and sharp bends. Grass-covered farmland hid behind stonewalls that lined the road as he trundled ever downwards, crunching through the gears to help brake the engine. Evidence of Rosedale's industrial past lay in the giant roasting kilns from the ironstone mines set above the village looking more like a crumbling viaduct than anything else. He'd walked with Jade along the path of the old railway many times and seen these imposing furnaces up close, drawn in by the sheer beauty and stillness that enveloped the dale.

Winding down the window, he breathed in the fresh air and sheer tranquillity of the place. The beauty of the countryside around him soothed his mind, distracting him from what might lie ahead.

He weaved past the village green and parked the car next to the churchyard. The tower of the old Cistercian Priory poked up near one of the church doors, the only remnant of Henry VIII's dissolution of the monasteries. He wondered what the nuns who'd lived there would think about the bulk of their treasured building being knocked down and the stones reused to build the current church. As it was used for another religious purpose, he guessed they wouldn't mind.

Leaving the rest of the travelling party inside, he made his way through the iron gate and headed for a tall man trimming the grass from the ancient gravestones.

As Turner approached, the man smiled in greeting and shouldered his shears. He took in the visitor's loud Hawaiian shirt and assumed, wrongly, that Turner was an American tourist. They'd had a lot coming through lately on historic tours of the moors. He didn't mind. The subsequent spending in the gift shops and cafes was a great boost to the local community. He reached out his hand and Turner shook it warmly. Then he beckoned towards the church and said, 'It's open if you want to look around.'

Turner shook his head. 'I'm looking for an old vicarage around here. I'm supposed to be meeting a friend there but the satnav has packed up,' he lied. 'My friend told me it has a gravel drive and a lot of trees around it. And there's a weathervane on the roof in the shape of a griffin. Is there anything like that around here, or have I gone completely wrong?' He held his breath, waiting for a reply.

Surprised by the man's northern accent, the graveyard gardener felt downhearted that his visitor was not there to part with some much-needed cash. 'Yes, sure. Up on the hill at the edge of the village. Does your friend live there? It's a private dwelling now, so if you've come on a sightseeing tour I'm afraid you won't be able to go in.'

Assuring him that his imaginary friend did indeed live there, Turner pressed for directions before the tall man could quiz him about the name of his friend, how long he'd known him or anything else that would expose his lie. In this small-knit community, it was probable that the amiable gardener knew who lived there and Turner didn't want to take the chance. Waving his thanks and goodbyes, he headed swiftly back to the car.

Lee still shuffled through the papers on his lap as Turner started the car and headed up the winding road that led out of the pretty village.

Tony leant forward from the back, resting his toned forearms on top of both seats. 'Well – have you got anything?' He tilted his head to listen for the reply over the sound of the engine.

Concentrating on the road, Turner said, 'Maybe. I'm not sure. Apparently, there's a place on the outskirts of the village that meets the description.'

Glancing ahead, Tony stayed propped forward and scanned every building they passed like a wide-eyed hawk.

After just over a mile of climbing they came across a large stone wall with an imposing black gate in the middle, and a sign that read 'Vicarage Cottage – Private Property'. Turner pulled the car to one side of the gate and motioned everybody to get out.

Free of his metal prison at last, Kyle sniffed at the air, stretched out his legs and yawned, before bounding up to Turner, panting, wondering what exciting game was in store.

Turner stroked the fur at the nape of Kyle's neck and clipped him on the lead.

'Right, here's the plan. We all go in with Kyle in front. If we get stopped, we say we're out walking the dog and we thought the grounds were a public footpath, or something like that, and apologise.'

It was the best Turner could think of on the spur of the moment, and he hoped it would stick if they were confronted by an angry tenant wondering who the hell this weird-looking bunch of trespassers were.

Nodding in agreement, the group set off through the creaking gate, their footsteps crunching on the gravel drive.

Tony secured the ASP baton to a pouch on his belt and pulled his T-shirt over it so it couldn't be seen. Used to police raids, he suggested they split up and circle the building, then meet around the other side to regroup.

He gazed up at the large stone face of the building; it was hard to guess its actual size. Splitting up would help them cover more ground quickly, giving them less chance of discovery and a quick exit if they didn't find anything suspicious.

A curving bay window at the front overlooked the lawn and mature trees that served as the boundary of the property. On the other side of the central front door a small window offered the same view. All the curtains were open, so they'd need to be careful not to disturb the owners – assuming they were at home, of course.

Upstairs, the same natural oak window frames sat directly over their lower counterparts. Varnish peeled away from the wood. The whole place looked downtrodden and uncared for. Perched bizarrely on the top of the brick chimney pot was a battered weathervane in the shape of a griffin.

Feeling he was finally on the right track, Turner picked up the pace, his heart hammering in his chest.

Turner set off with Kyle around the left of the building, keeping clear of the view from the windows as far as possible. He pulled the dog onto the grass, away from the gravel, so as to hide the sound of their movement. Everything looked normal. An old rusty wheelbarrow had been carelessly upended against the wall. Stopping to listen, he could hear no noise from the inside and he felt self-conscious about intruding on the privacy of what were, more than likely, law-abiding citizens of the village. He made his way furtively around the back, and reined Kyle back to his side as a grey squirrel crossed ahead and shot up an oak tree.

At the rear, more gravel provided a car-parking area. Two large garages with huge solid wood doors stood at the end of the garden. Again, the garages had seen better days – the window lights above the doors were largely cracked and broken. Turner saw Lee and Tony appear around the other side of the house and both shrugged to tell him they'd found nothing unusual.

Turner motioned them to stay where they were and moved quietly to the first garage; the door was slightly ajar. Up close, he could now see a heating duct that travelled around the side of the building before disappearing underground. Easing the door open took much of his strength and he tried to do it slowly so as to keep the noise down as it slid across the stones below.

A wave of humidity hit him as he peered inside. The window lights painted the interior in a soft glow and Turner could make out a large muddy area at the front that seemed to disappear into a wide pool at the back. In the mud, a snaking line left the water and headed towards the door with what looked like huge clawed footprints at regular intervals either side. There was a strange musky smell of earth and decaying vegetation overpowered by another unmistakeable scent – rotting fish. The source sat in a stinking bucket of what looked like mackerel, piled high. Even more bizarrely, half a dozen chicken carcasses had been strung above the bucket and tied off to hooks in the wall. What the hell? thought Turner, pulling back on the dog as it tried to get at the fish in the bucket. This looked like a bizarre enclosure for a beast that fed on raw fish and meat, one that that wasn't particularly fussy about how fresh its food was. Turner sighed with relief; whatever lived in that strange dwelling didn't appear to be at home at the moment.

He headed back outside and around the back of the garage towards a green tarpaulin thrown over something just over half his height and leaning to one side. Carefully he lifted up the corner, pulling the dog in tight to his hip, and peered underneath. There was no need to lift the rest of the sheet; he already knew what it was from his brief glance.

Hugh Williams's scooter.

CHAPTER 20 – TEA AND CAKE

Turner motioned the others to meet him at the front of the house, and sprinted across the lawn, the dog enjoying the adventure at his side. There was no need for secrecy now. If Williams *were* in there, then paying a call on his old friend would be a natural thing to do. There would likely be questions about how Turner knew where Williams lived, but the psychic felt sure he could bluff his way through that. Until he had more information about why the princess had directed him here, Turner felt he needed to play it straight. However, this seemed too much of a coincidence and he wondered whether the princess had been playing games with him. Why, he had no idea.

He shooed the others behind him and knocked on the front door. Up close, there was more evidence of peeling varnish and the wood showed bare in patches around the handle. After what seemed like an age, soft footsteps could be heard coming down a passage. A curious Williams opened the door.

A brief wave of fear washed over Williams's face as he took in the crowd of people on his doorstep, quickly replaced by his customary smile. His ability to deal with the unexpected was extraordinary and Turner could only assume it had spawned from his years on the stage.

'Well, this is a surprise. Come in, please – welcome to my humble abode,' Williams said, waving his arms to beckon them inside.

What a pro, thought Turner for the umpteenth time. There was no 'What are you doing here?' or 'How did you find me?' He acted for all the world like he'd expected them to call.

Williams moved through the wide hall with its imposing central staircase and ushered them into the side room with the large bay window facing the front lawn. The decoration looked like a comfortable Edwardian squire rented the place. Two wicker chairs sat either side of the window, and a light chintz settee faced the fireplace. Floral curtains draped back to gold-threaded tiebacks secured on shiny brass knobs. The fire looked cold, and the feel of the room was more of a life-size doll's house rather than a real place for humans to stretch out in. It smelled musty and unlived in; the light streaming in from the window highlighting the dust sparkling and twisting in the air currents.

Williams bustled away and returned with a huge pot of tea and delicate china cups, still smiling as he placed the tray on the low table next to the settee. 'Please gentlemen, be my guest.' He scurried away again to fetch some cake.

The whole thing felt surreal to the visitors, as if they'd stepped back in time to a bygone era of good manners and gentlemen callers.

Returning with a mountain of cake and a bone for the dog, Williams appeared to visibly relax and pulled over one of the wicker chairs from the window.

There the visitors sat, crammed on the settee, at their feet the dog gnawing at the bone, facing their genial host. It was like a pleasant domestic scene from a period piece – an Edwardian movie where the set designer had forgotten to tell the costume department what they should be wearing.

Turner did the introductions and after a few slurps and a mouthful of cake said, 'Sorry to surprise you like this. We were in the area, so it just seemed natural to stop by.'

Williams seemed to accept the lie without a thought and mentioned how nice it was to have company. Now Turner knew they were both lying. The twitching at the corner of Williams's eye suggested the last thing he wanted was company. Or maybe he was nervous; certainly, he was trying desperately to keep a mask on his true emotions.

Pushing his fingers together to stop them twitching, Williams said, 'It's good to be back home after roughing it in the caravan, but I'm only here to pick up some clean clothes before I head back to Hunmanby. You're lucky to catch me. I guess you got this address from my business card.'

Turner nodded, remembering that the clairvoyant had written the details of his caravan plot on the back of one of his cards. He hoped the excuse would stick – the thought that a vicarage address was on the other side of the business card had never occurred to him, but he played along, still wondering why the princess had drawn him here.

Appearing satisfied with the explanation, Williams smiled. 'But you haven't brought your wife. Is this a boy's day out, then?'

But behind the smile was panic. Turner could feel it.

There was something going on in this house that Williams didn't want them to know about, though his acting skills were remarkable. Turner sensed that Williams already knew Jade was missing. More than that, he felt that his genial host had played a part in it. Why he thought that he didn't know, as the clairvoyant had done nothing so far but try to help in his own way. Turner's intuition was hardly ever wrong, though, and he leant forward to probe further.

Before Turner could speak, Lee chimed in to support his friend's story. 'That's right. It's just us men on the road today. When we realised we'd driven close to where you lived we thought we'd drop in and see if you were home,' he said, trying his best to support the lie and look relaxed. Unsure what else to do, and unwilling to make eye contact with Williams, Lee took a large mouthful of cake. Crumbs littered Lee's T-shirt as though he were expecting a flock of birds to have a picnic on it.

Tony sipped his tea, looking Williams up and down as only a detective could. He'd spotted the same nervousness in their host, well hidden behind the mask, but definitely there. The same look he'd seen a thousand times in a police interview room.

Williams stood and walked over to the window. He gazed out into the garden and thrust his hands in his pockets to hide the trembling. 'It's a beautiful place. I've only been here a few months – I haven't even had time to decorate.'

Turner guessed the move to look outside was so he didn't have to face his guests. There was an air of unease growing in the man, as if he were waiting for something that hadn't happened yet.

Lee brushed the crumbs from his T-shirt onto the pale chintz of the settee and grabbed another piece of cake. 'I like it. Makes me feel like I'm a guest in Downton Abbey.' The guitarist was no good at deceit and he was over-talking to cover the guilt he felt inside.

Glancing across to Lee, Turner tried to signal him to shut the hell up so he could get on with questioning Williams. Lee's social-interaction filter, even when he wasn't lying, had never been good, and he tended to treat everyone he met like one of his old band mates. That was fine for their circle of friends but letting him loose in polite society could be a major embarrassment. Turner had found this out to his cost when doing a reading, albeit a fake one, for a prestigious lady of means who'd been awarded an MBE for her charity work and called in at his house. Lee had strolled past the seated pair in the lounge wearing only his underpants, saying, 'All right, luv?' to his guest before grabbing a cigar and heading back into his bedroom.

The glare from Turner was enough to make Lee clam up. Next to him, Tony began to sway in his chair, rocking backwards and forwards, squinting as if struggling to see. Something was desperately wrong and Turner felt a warning bell going off in his brain, demanding his attention. Down on the floor, the dog had rolled on its side and dozed heavily, its tongue flopping unnaturally.

Swinging back to face his visitors, Williams said, 'When we moved in we spent all our money just to buy the place.' The hands were out of the pockets now and confidence had returned to his face.

The room began to pulse in and out. Slowly, Turner

struggled to his feet. 'You said "we". What do you mean "we"? I didn't know you were in a relationship.' His voice seemed distant and unconnected. Desperately, he tried to focus his blurring vision on his host.

Williams sat looking at his guests as if he were observing rats in a laboratory experiment. There was a cold detachment mixed with curiosity and perhaps even fear. He stood to face the swaying frame of Turner. 'You'll find out soon enough, Nathen. Please forgive me – I've got no choices left,' he said softly, catching the psychic as he fell forward into his arms.

Behind him, Tony and Lee had collapsed onto each other and were propped awkwardly against the back of the settee. Drool trickled from Lee's mouth, staining Tony's T-shirt.

Panting under the weight, Williams dropped Turner heavily onto the floor. Cursing under his breath, he reminded himself to increase the dose of the drug in the tea next time. This had taken far too long and stretched his nerves to breaking point. At least it looked like he'd got it right in the dog's bone, he thought, as he headed out the door like a man with the world on his shoulders.

CHAPTER 21 – AN UNHAPPY REUNION

The wood-lined room smelled of linseed oil and leather. Painted portraits, hanging either side of a huge curtained alcove, gazed down unemotionally at a female figure draped head to toe in black lace with a veil over her face; opposite sat a man in a loud Hawaiian shirt. In the corner, a large dresser had been pushed away from the wall, exposing a concrete hole underneath.

Slowly, Turner lifted his head and wished he hadn't. The room spun in front of him, and at the centre of this whirlpool he could see a veiled figure clothed in black. Deep in his blurred memories something stirred. He'd seen the figure before. The name Molly Craggs surfaced and he remembered his vision after he'd summoned her spirit. Then there was the description from the fishmonger of the same person in black, the one who'd last been seen with Jade. Remembering his wife's name stirred other thoughts. Missing. She was missing and he'd set out to find her. Everything came flooding back to him and he jolted upright. Trying to stand, he toppled over and fell, hitting his head with a crack on the wooden floor. Across the room someone dashed to help him. Turner kicked and struggled to his feet, swaying like a drunk in a gale. Blood trickled from his forehead and sent waves of pain through his body.

The figure that had pushed him back in his chair said, 'Sit, Nathen, sit. This will all be over soon.'

He recognised the voice. Squinting, he made out the face. Williams. He tried to stand again, but his legs wouldn't support him, and he still had no memory of how he'd got into this position.

Walking behind the lace figure, Williams said, 'Please just stay in your chair. It's for your own safety. Don't worry about your friends – they're locked away, dozing in the front room.'

Turner tried to make sense of it all. He needed time to allow his fogged senses to return. Desperately thinking of a way to stall, he tried to speak but no words came. Concentrating hard, he took another stab at it. Nothing. His body felt like he'd been on an alcoholic binge but had avoided the typical aftermath of a dry mouth and desiccated organs craving rehydration. Focusing his attention on his breathing, he inhaled deeply, counted to ten in his head, then let the breath ease out with another ten count. After a few cycles, the extra oxygen helped revive him and calm his growing panic.

At last he found his voice. 'What the hell's going on? What have you done to me?' The words sounded hollow in his head, as if he were speaking from inside a tunnel.

Across the room, Williams looked at the floor and then patted the veiled figure on the shoulders. 'Look, I didn't want this. She made me do it. I had to dose your tea with chloral hydrate. I'm so sorry. Just relax and everything will work out for the best, okay?'

Feeling far from relaxed, Turner tried to focus his vision on the clairvoyant, who stood shifting his body weight from side to side as if trying to keep his balance on a rolling ship. Turner had heard of chloral hydrate, one of the so-called date-rape drugs, and read many sorry cases in the newspapers about its consequences. Irrationally, he looked down to see if he was still wearing his trousers. He was, and breathed a croaking sigh of relief.

At least the drug explained the mire clouding his brain. Blinking rapidly to focus his vision, he looked around the room, trying to take it all in. Spotting the concrete hole in the floor didn't help his growing feelings of unease.

As if sensing what he was looking at, Williams said, 'Don't worry about that. It's just an old priest hole left over from when the house was built. We're going to get it filled in.'

After years studying many cults and mainstream religions, Turner was aware that the older homes for the clergy often held a variety of boltholes for their tenants to hide in should they have been pursued by puritanical fanatics in darker, less tolerant times. It still didn't explain why the dresser used to cover it had been moved away. Was Williams intending to dump him in the priest hole? Was this revenge for exposing him as a fraud?

But there was something else. Williams kept saying *we* and Turner assumed that the lady clothed in black was the other referred to. Straining his eyes, he scanned the woman seated in the chair but she faded in and out like he was looking through a camera with a faulty autofocus.

Moving around to stand at the side of the black-clad

figure, Williams picked up the edge of the veil with trembling fingers. The twitch at the corner of his eye was back and he seemed hesitant, reluctant even, as if he were an unwilling extra in a morbid charade.

'Is this the person you're looking for? The one that you believe is responsible for the attack on Sandra Vaughan and the death of Molly Craggs. Is that why you came here today?'

Clenching his teeth, Turner could feel the metallic taste of blood in his mouth, trickling down his face from the wound on his forehead. How could Williams know about the lady swathed in black he was hunting? He'd never told him about it. There was only one way – Williams must be part of it all. What Turner had sensed during their genial tea conversation was correct. The thought sickened him.

This con man had strung him along all the way. He planned to find out why. And find out quickly. If Williams was in on this, then he must know where Jade was. Of course Turner wanted to meet the veiled woman doing her best impression of the corpse bride, but he didn't want to let his true emotions show. Not sure of his next move, he sat quietly, trying to buy time to recover his senses.

A shadowy shape at the back of the room had seen enough. Previously unnoticed in the gloom of the wood-lined prison, the figure stepped into the light.

'Hello again, Nathen. I knew you'd come.'

The voice was soft, child-like even. Turner recognised it immediately. It was Princess Amunet.

'I did wonder whether I'd given you enough clues at the psychic fair. But you're a very resourceful man, aren't you, Nathen Turner?'

In the last words, there was a venom that Turner hadn't heard before. The voice seemed to change down to a regular speaking voice, away from the soothing style he'd heard previously.

'Don't you know who I am?' she said, all pretence of softness gone. The princess stepped closer.

Looking at the smooth features and beautiful almond eyes, of course he knew. But the voice had changed. This voice belonged to someone from his past. No, it couldn't be, he thought, taking in every feature of the flawless complexion. Again, he had a sense that her words were slightly out of sync with her lips.

Moving to stand next to the veiled figure in black, the princess said, 'I'm sure you know who this is.' She pulled back the veil on the seated figure with a mocking grin on her face.

Sitting close to death in the chair was Jade, a strip of gaffer tape stuck over her mouth. Turner noticed the manacles around her feet and wrists as they glistened in the dull overhead lamp. It was impossible to tell from this distance if she was still breathing, and he panicked. Trying to rush across the room, his legs buckled underneath him and he fell down hard again on the wooden floor.

Motioning Williams to one side, the princess crouched down to look into Turner's eyes, making sure she had his full and undivided attention before continuing. She wanted to relish this moment. A moment she'd dreamt about for years. Reaching behind the chair for a bamboo walking stick, she flicked back her braids and stood to tower over him.

'I loved you Nathen, I really did.' Using the walking stick

as a support, she lowered herself to the floor. She smiled into Turner's bloody face, kissed him on the cheek and stroked his hair. 'You used to say I was so pretty, didn't you?'

The battered psychic struggled to understand how this voice from his past, one that he knew so well, came from a completely different person. Looking into the eyes for some clue, he simply nodded, stalling for time, trying to figure out what it all meant.

The princess reached up to her crown, yanked hard at the braided hair and rocked her head backwards and forwards. Her features slithered upwards, bit by straining bit. The lips seemed to melt together as the silicone mask was eased over the face and crumpled into her hand.

Leaning forward, nose-to-nose with Turner and now unmasked, she said, 'Look at me now, Nathen. Do you still think I'm pretty?'

As the horror in front of his eyes faded into blackness, Turner heard himself screaming as he collapsed on the floor.

CHAPTER 22 – THE VOICE OF A DEMON

Silence filled the room as if a darkness had descended and smothered it of all life. Damp from the wood-lined walls wafted the odour of decay across to Turner. As he regained consciousness, he eased his body upright and gazed into the gloom. Across from him, his wife sat in an unnatural posture, as if a string puppet in a black dress had been dropped onto a chair. Behind her, Williams flinched, backing towards the wall as he looked over at the prone figure in the loud shirt with pity. Nothing about the way Williams stood suggested he wanted to be there.

Then the face that had horrified Turner came back into view. The skin was mottled with red and white scar tissue, thick folds of flesh pulled taut around the eyes, giving them a slanted appearance. There were no earlobes or hair to speak of, but that wasn't the worst thing. Around the mouth and jawline, a huge jagged gash sliced through to the bone on the left side, exposing yellowing teeth underneath. The overall impression was of a bloody skull that had been coated in blobs of red and white modelling clay. The skull began to speak, spittle oozing through the gaps in the flesh, making the voice lisp badly without the constraint of the Egyptian mask. 'Do you still think I'm pretty, Nathen?'

One emotion pushed through the horror that filled Turner's mind – pity. Looking directly at the scarred features, he could still see the traces of the woman as she'd once been. The beautiful golden hair had gone, the dainty features replaced by this scarred abomination. A woman he'd cared for and loved. What she must have been through, how she must have suffered, he thought. It was Zoe, Williams's sister, the one who'd brought Williams and him together all those years ago. They'd shared wonderful times of laughter and companionship and now it had come to this. Struggling to reconcile that Princess Amunet and the ghoulish apparition were one and the same person made his head spin. No wonder she'd recognised him at the psychic fair – she knew him intimately.

'W-What happened to you? What's all this about? I never meant to hurt you, Zoe.'

Trying again to spook him, Zoe swung her head so Turner could see the gruesome gash in the cheek up close. 'I needed you, Nathen. You were my world, remember?'

Turner did remember, though he'd say he'd been less her world, more her possession. That had been the start of their issues as she'd increasingly tried to control him. Speaking to another woman back then had sent her into a jealous fit of rage. And that was before her drug-induced psychosis had kicked in, caused by the chemical soup of anti-depressants she'd been taking. But Williams had told him after the psychic show that she was a lot better now. At least, that is, when she remembered to take her medication. The maimed person glaring in front of him was certainly not better; she was clearly unhinged and he'd need to be careful. The thought of what she might have already done, and what she planned to do next, made his skin crawl as he looked at the mangled features.

'I tried to forget about you,' said Zoe. 'Put it behind me. But then, out of nowhere, you sit calmly in front of me at the clairvoyant show, sporting this slut on your arm.' Zoe pointed back at Jade, and Turner thought she was going to hit her.

Chills shivered down Turner's spine as he realised that Zoe had gone completely insane. Memories of the psychic fair pushed into his mind – the strange scent he'd detected when he'd stood to leave the princess. A new-car smell that he'd dismissed without a second thought. What he'd detected was the faint odour of the silicone Egyptian mask up close. Should he have known? Could he have known? he wondered, frantically trying to piece together the clues in the trail that had led him to this. The way the lips of the princess had seemed out of sync at times when she spoke – it was because of the mask. But her acting skills were extraordinary, as though she had different personas inside her that she could inhabit at will. Maybe she wasn't acting, Turner thought anxiously. Maybe these different personalities really did live in the same body. At least in her deranged mind, anyway. Williams had tried to warn him that his stage partner was a little crazy, had told him not to bother contacting her. But he'd refused to listen, so obsessed was he that she did have true spiritual insight. Realising that Williams might have been an unwitting participant in this bizarre charade, that he'd been trying to help his sister work through her demented state of mind, didn't make Turner feel any warmer towards the clairvoyant. Quite the opposite – had Williams spoken up and told the truth earlier, then perhaps all this mayhem could have been avoided.

Lifting his head to look across at Williams, Turner said, 'You knew all about this, didn't you? Why didn't you say anything? How the hell can it have come to this? You could have told me. We could have sat down and talked ...'

Before he could say anymore, Zoe slapped Turner viciously across the cheek, causing stars to pop and burst in front of his eyes.

With eyes gleaming, Zoe giggled and looked at her brother. 'Because I told him not to. You always do what I say, don't you, little brother?'

Across the room, Williams stood with his head bowed and refused to meet Turner's gaze. Slowly, he nodded, causing another cackle of glee from his sister.

The unmasked face of horror moved closer, still wondering why the psychic wasn't gagging or retching like everyone else who saw her mutilated features. 'You dumped me right before Christmas, remember? Talk about timing. Do you know what it's like, sitting there alone on Christmas day when all your family and friends are away? Well, I do. To know nobody cares about you on the one day of the year that's supposed to spread love and happiness to all men.' Zoe slapped Turner again, harder this time.

Unsure what Zoe might be capable of in her current state of mind, Turner tried to keep her talking, hoping it might calm her. Backing up to sit in the empty chair, he hoped he was now out of range if Zoe tried to strike him again.

'But I still don't understand. How did you come to look

like this? What's all this about?' Turner genuinely wanted to know what had happened to this creature he'd once loved. The thought that he'd been responsible in some way didn't sit well on his conscience. Rubbing at his cheek, he felt the skin glowing red under his touch.

Zoe pulled back to look at him. There was genuine concern on his face and the fire of hatred that burned inside her shrank briefly. 'I fell asleep. Sitting on my own watching TV. All those sickening Christmas messages of comfort and joy blaring out made me drink heavily. I passed out and slumped on the table. You know my old flat, Nathen – I always kept scented candles burning.' The memories became vivid in her mind and tears welled in the folds of skin underneath her eyes.

Turner remembered her place well – he'd been there often enough. At the time, Zoe had been into the hippy culture, obsessed with a peculiar mixture of philosophies and ideas about science and religion. Her flat had been like an air-freshener factory, the rooms always filled with the scent of burning joss sticks or some fancy candle she'd picked up in the market.

Zoe sat down cross-legged in front of him, put the bamboo walking stick she'd been carrying on the floor and placed her hands on his thigh.

Not knowing what else to do, Turner reached over and covered them with his own. At least if he covered her hands it would prevent another stinging blow, he thought.

Feeling the warmth of his palms, she looked up and remembered the gentle giant she'd once loved. Her mania lessened and with a trembling voice, she said, 'My hair caught light on one of the candles. I woke up screaming but by then it was too late. The flames had spread to my clothing and – well, you can see the result.'

Leaning over, Turner spoke softly, tears welling in his eyes. 'I'm so sorry, Zoe. If I'd known, I could've helped. Why didn't you tell—'

'My neighbour heard me screaming and used her spare key to get into the flat. She saved my life, but for what? A plastic surgeon convinced me he could restore the damage and bring back my looks. You see the result of his handiwork.' She pointed to the gash on her cheek. 'The idiot didn't realise the flesh was so badly damaged he couldn't patch it. I went from burn victim to ghoul.'

Stepping forward, Williams leant down to cradle his sister, who sobbed openly now. 'I did try and contact you, Nathen, but you were off touring with your psychic show. It left me alone and I tried to help as much as I could. One of the guys I met when I worked on the cruise lines was this Hollywood special-effects expert. We got talking about my dad, who'd been in the trade, and, well, one thing led to another and he offered to help.'

Turner felt sick inside as he realised his ex-lover must've been through hell while he was out on the road, scamming the public for a living. Trying to push away the guilt and shame that pricked at his conscience, he focused hard as Williams explained how they'd travelled down to a special-effects workshop in London while his new friend was in town, shooting yet another Hollywood remake of *The Mummy*. After taking a life cast of Zoe's mutilated features they'd made a couple of moulds and then added the face from one of the movie's Egyptian extras. They had nothing else to go on. No way of matching what Zoe had looked like before the disfigurement without extensive, and expensive computer-modelling based on old photographs. This particular favour was not in his new friend's budget capability.

Williams picked up the Egyptian mask that lay discarded on the floor and held it up to Turner. 'You see – it's a fabulous piece of work. This guy is a miracle worker. It fools everyone.'

Inside, Williams felt again the joy of being able to help his disfigured sibling. But this willingness to please her had now taken him down a dark and dangerous path. One that he'd never expected, and that he wanted no part in.

Looking at the sagging features of the mask, Turner had to admit it had completely fooled him. But he felt ashamed. As a man who prided himself on a so-called psychic sixth sense to pick up on things others missed, he'd completely misunderstood the signals. The fear and sense of connection with the princess had confused him at the time – well, he wasn't confused anymore. He felt responsible. Had he spotted the signs when he'd first seen her at Williams's show, all this carnage could have been avoided. Turner felt, no, he knew, that if he'd discovered the deception earlier he could have talked to Zoe ... reasoned with her and offered to help in some way.

What else could they be hiding from him and what had they already done? he wondered apprehensively. Feeling utterly despondent, Turner dropped his chin to his chest and braced himself for more ravings from his captors.

Over in the corner, Zoe pulled on the mask of the princess, inch by slow inch, and moulded it to her face. Thank God, thought Turner, unkindly, but glad to be free of the vision of the damaged features. Having not managed to get the fit quite right, Zoe's mouth sagged at the corners as she spoke. 'They gave me chloral hydrate to help me sleep,' she said, lisping badly, 'but they couldn't help the pain and loss I felt inside. But then I was saved, reborn into a new life, a new beginning.'

Moving over to the curtained alcove between the two paintings at the end of the room, Zoe pulled on a rope at the side. The curtains slid back. At the rear of the recess, wall-mounted candles illuminated an elaborate painting with three panels that glittered in the light. The first panel showed a bizarre creature with the rear legs and round behind of a hippo, the front legs of a lion and the snarling head of a crocodile travelling on a long wooden boat. The surrounding sea was on fire and filled with clawing demons that reached up, trying to drag the boat under. On the second panel, the crocodile-headed creature was in a mortal struggle with an enormous serpent that slithered and coiled its body around the struggling beast. In the last one, the creature was transformed and reborn, first as a griffin, then as a falcon, and finally as a scarab beetle, crawling across a sand dune into a new dawn. Above the painting a shimmering circular disc flickered golden rays across the scene.

'These are sacred scenes of rebirth, Nathen. My rebirth – to return this time not as the ghoul of a woman I once was, but as a princess.'

Turner was already well acquainted with ancient

Egyptian mythology and religious beliefs, and recognised the scenes of rebirth at once. But he knew that these scenes always featured a heroic pharaoh figure, not the strange crocodile-headed beast in the illustrations. But that was not what drew his attention.

In the middle of the alcove was a large rectangular granite shrine about four feet tall and two feet across. Inside the hollow shrine stood a golden statue of the crocodile-headed creature illustrated in the panels, its mouth open, sharp teeth gleaming in the light. Turner didn't need to see it any closer; he'd already recognised it as the figure of the ancient Egyptian demon Ammit, the so-called devourer of the dead. According to the various accounts he'd read, Ammit had epitomised divine retribution in ancient Egypt. The creature devoured the hearts of those unworthy to pass into the afterlife, and left their souls doomed to wander restlessly for an eternity. At the feet of the figure lay several wax dolls about the length of a human palm, and on the top of the shrine an oil lamp burned under a copper brazier. This bizarre vision of ancient Egypt, set in a quiet country vicarage, firmly confirmed to Turner that both of his captors were completely out of their minds. Cold sweat oozed from his pores, staining his shirt, as he wondered what horrors would unfold next.

Zoe lifted the statue of Ammit and cradled it in her palm. 'I cried myself to sleep night after night after you left me. But then I realised I needed to be reborn as someone else if I was to move forward with my life. Leave the old Zoe behind and find a new path. I'd already been reborn in a way with the Egyptian mask. So I studied all the texts I could find on rebirth in ancient Egypt, hoping they'd help me find an answer.' She stroked the scaly head of the statue, running her fingers over the sharp teeth. 'As if to answer my prayers, the voice of Ammit spoke to me in my dreams. He called out to me and told me I was to be reborn as Amunet, a name like his own. The name means "the female hidden one" in Egyptian.' Picking up one of the wax figures from the shrine and motioning to the copper brazier, she said, 'These are my life, my resurrection. Hidden in the wax are the sacred spells of rebirth. Every morning I burn one and I am born again as a beautiful Egyptian princess.'

Williams stood sheepishly to the side. Surely he knew she was crazy, Turner thought, convinced that drug-induced hallucinations had brought on Zoe's mania and the voice of Ammit in her head. Thinking about what exactly this demon in the form of a golden statue would tell her to do next made Turner shudder inside.

Placing the statue and the wax figure reverently back on the shrine, Zoe said, 'Everything I have done is in Ammit's name. The doctors told me I was hallucinating and hearing things because of the drugs I'd been taking. But I knew different. Ammit was there when I needed help the most, and has been with me ever since. Look at me now.' As if to emphasise her words, Zoe pirouetted on the spot and glanced at Turner with a crooked grin.

Looking back towards the shrine, Zoe smiled at the statue that stared across the room. 'I was finally happy, creating a new future on the stage and putting the past behind me. But then you crashed back into my life at the clairvoyant show with that tart on your arm.' Zoe spat the last words in Turner's face, then looked across at Jade's motionless body with pure hatred in her eyes. 'I locked myself in my campervan after the show and spoke to Ammit. Ammit always knows the right path, the right words to soothe me.'

Moving past Jade, Williams picked up the bamboo walking stick that his sister had placed on the floor and swung it through the air. Panic ripped through Turner, thinking Williams was about to strike his wife.

Jade still hadn't moved. Was he too late? Was she dead already? The shaking voice of Williams cut through his thoughts. 'Zoe had been told by the voice of Ammit that if she killed Jade, you'd be a free man again and you'd come running back to her.'

No, I wouldn't, you crazy lunatic, Turner thought, but remained quiet.

'You have to believe me, Nathen. I had no idea things would come to this. I just thought listening to her wild fantasies would soothe her. How was I to know she intended to act on them? All I've been doing is trying to help; she's never acted on her fantasies before. But now I'm involved, don't you see? There's no choice for me now but to see this thing through. Zoe attacked Sandra Vaughan by mistake, thinking she was Jade.'

Oh my God, thought Turner. He'd seen Zoe in her princess guise cradling a statue in the lighted living area of the campervan after the clairvoyant show. Something Williams had explained away as her need to meditate, cleanse her spirit and seek guidance after a performance. Now he knew exactly what that guidance was and he felt nauseated, realising his appearance at the show with Jade on his arm had triggered all this. Stirring Zoe's memories had fuelled an unquenchable thirst for revenge – the final straw that had broken her mind and pushed her delusions into lethal action.

Zoe sank to the floor, sobbing, and grabbed Turner's wrists. 'I'm so sorry, Nathen. You understand, don't you?' She shook his wrists, pleading with him. 'I'd been watching your house and then I saw Jade – or at least I thought it was her – leave and head onto the beach. I'd never seen Jade up close before and the hair and figure looked the same, so I put on some old walking clothes and pretended to fall on the rocks. She came to help me and ...'

A glint of silver flashed in the lamp as Williams pulled at the handle on the bamboo walking stick to reveal a rectangular sword blade. 'And then Zoe attacked her with this,' Williams said, his shoulders sagging as he held the blade. The innocent-looking walking stick was an antique, and lethal, sword cane.

It was true, Jade and Sandra did look similar from a distance after Sandra had dyed her hair black, but accepting this didn't bring Turner any comfort. He tried not to think about the horror Sandra had been through, knowing that he must keep control of the emotions rattling through his brain if he was to find a way out of this. Somehow, he must figure out how to save his wife and bring these maniacs to justice.

'But what about Molly Craggs? How does her death fit in?' At least if he had all the facts he could give the information to the police, assuming he left this room alive.

More sobbing came from the floor. Through rattling breaths, Zoe said, 'It was an accident. Ammit told me that first I must seek out this woman, and get her help to find out Jade's movements. Then I could get your slut of a wife alone and kill her. I saw you and Molly hugging in the car park after the clairvoyant show, so I knew you must be close friends and that she'd know your daily routines. I went round to Molly's flat early the following morning to ask her about you, pretending to be an old woman collecting for charity. We keep all the addresses of people we've worked with and their family's details, so it was easy to find her. She told me she'd just met you, but I didn't believe her. Then she lifted the veil covering my face. When she saw me in the Egyptian mask, she said I wasn't old at all and accused me of conning her. She went crazy and ... well ... I reacted badly. All I wanted to do was talk to her.' The sobbing stopped abruptly and Zoe raised herself up on her knees and looked Turner in the eye. 'Don't think ill of me, Nathen. It was an accident – you have to believe me. Ammit told me my actions were pure because they were spawned from my pure heart.'

Wet eyes pleaded with him but Turner had gone cold inside. Coming across an angry Molly Craggs was not something he'd wish on anybody, but no one he knew would stoop to murder her. She'd died from a rectangular puncture wound straight through her body. Believing that thrusting a sword cane through Molly's chest was some sort of unfortunate accident was crazy. In any sane person's eyes that was cold-blooded murder, not self-defence. Plus, the thought that Zoe believed she'd acted from a pure heart was really twisted. It was obviously the actions of a deranged mind that sought lethal revenge on an ex-lover. Trying to justify those actions by saying they were the wishes of an imaginary voice was absurd.

The Egyptian face pleaded with him to understand. 'After I left Molly, I counted on you still living in the same place as when we were together, and I headed straight there. I didn't know what else to do. Then I saw what I thought was Jade leaving and I followed her to the beach. But I'd got the wrong person.'

Looking into Turner's eyes, Zoe searched for the forgiveness she so desperately craved. When she couldn't read his thoughts, it was as if a switch had turned off in her mind and she stood up, all emotion gone.

'I didn't feel I should go near your house again after what had happened on the beach, so I waited around the streets of Whitby, hoping I'd spot Jade. And then, as if by some miracle, she appeared with your dog. It was like it was meant to be. But I didn't want any more accidents, so I brought Jade back to the vicarage so my brother could see her and make sure I'd got the right person this time. He'd seen her up close during the show.'

Frightened by the abrupt change in Zoe's mood, Turner realised he needed help. Any help, in fact. Fumbling in his pocket for a handkerchief to wipe away the mixture of sweat and blood on his face, his fingers found the gold cross given to him by Molly's mother. Maybe he could try again to summon Molly's spirit, he thought desperately. A ghostly intervention might be enough to frighten the two siblings and send them running for cover. But he'd only been able to call on Molly's incorporeal being by burning some of the hair contained in the cross and then using his own abilities to summon her.

Looking at the granite altar, he had an idea. One that was unlikely to work, but he was out of options.

His thoughts were cut short as Zoe moved to a side panel in the alcove, slid back a bolt and called into the hole behind it.

'But now everything is as it should be and there'll be no more accidents,' she said, smiling back at Turner. 'Finally, we can finish what we started and all will be well again.'

A gentle rustle, followed by a wet sliding sound, made Turner stare as a calloused green snout eased out from the hole.

CHAPTER 23 – A LIFE IN THE BALANCE

Slithering with unblinking eyes into the gloom, the scaly shape inched forward. The same earthy smell that Turner had found in the garage outside filled his nostrils, and he gazed in terror as an enormous crocodile emerged into the light. Dark-bronze scales flickered in the glow from the candles as the beast made its way into the room. Around the wide neck was a steel collar attached to a chain that disappeared into the open panel in the wall.

Zoe called out to the giant reptile in soothing tones, but Turner noticed that she kept her distance from the gaping jaws. Taking a step back, she said, 'Meet Sobek, my pet and protector. My brother rescued her from a carnival act that had been closed down for animal cruelty. But I'm not cruel to you, am I, my darling?'

In response, the scaly face turned to scan the room as if looking for the next thing, or person, it would welcome into its enormous jaws. Drool dripped from its conical teeth and puddled on the floor.

Trembling, and unconsciously wrapping his arms around his body, Turner eased back in his chair. Looking into the cold eyes of the crocodile felt like staring into prehistory, to a time when huge reptiles had roamed the earth. Williams had told him that he'd got his sister a pet, but Turner had never imagined this monstrosity.

Seeming pleased with Turner's look of terror, Zoe crossed the floor to stand behind Jade. Placing her hands on Jade's shoulders she said, 'Now is the time for judgement, Nathen. In ancient times, crocodiles symbolised the plunge from the dry land of ordinary life into the flowing water of the afterlife.' Gazing across to the golden statue of Ammit in the shrine, she smiled and tilted her head back as if listening. 'Just as Ammit has told me, the hearts of the unworthy must be consumed. There's no escape from the sins of our mortal life.' Moving her hands from Jade's shoulders, she circled them around her neck. 'And this slut, this harlot, has sinned and now she will pay for it.'

Turner shouted across to Williams, who stood cowering in the corner. 'Hugh you've got to stop this … this is madness.'

Williams backed further away, looking like he was about to run out of the room. It was obvious he was terrified of the crocodile, and Turner wondered if it was the threat of the beast being turned on him that had kept him compliant with Zoe's wishes.

Flicking its tail excitedly, the crocodile moved towards Jade as far as the steel chain would allow.

Turner was desperate. He needed to do something, but he wasn't a fighter. The effect of the drug still swam through his brain and he felt drained and uncoordinated. Even if he tried to attempt anything physical it would be nothing short of suicide. Calling on all his years as a fake psychic medium, manipulating people for a living, he thought about how he might reframe the situation in the head of the unhinged sister and find a way to give her what she wanted. He needed to satisfy her desire to act on the obscene words of her imagined demon, Ammit, and present Zoe with the prize of love and affection she craved. Plus he'd thought of a vague, and more supernatural solution to scare his captors.

He spoke softly, so that Zoe had to concentrate to hear him, and pretended to act the part of a man making a life-changing decision after seeing the error of his ways.

'I do understand, and I'm sorry for my part in this. I don't care about what's happened to you. I know you're beautiful inside. None of this is your fault. You were only acting on what you believed, and what Ammit told you to do.'

Acting on misguided religious beliefs had led to the slaughter of millions of innocents throughout the years, he thought, but this was way too deranged. Playing the part of a consoling lover took all his strength, and his body shook with the effort. Looking across at the clairvoyant, Turner thought that Williams genuinely appeared shocked at what his sister had done; his face was ashen as he placed the sword cane on the floor, and he still looked like he was about to bolt.

Hearing the words she'd longed for, Zoe rushed over, threw her arms around Turner and kissed him on the mouth. The masked lips tasted like he'd chewed on a tyre, but he didn't recoil.

'I knew you'd understand, Nathen,' Zoe said. 'We were meant for each other. I always felt it in my heart. You know now that we must kill Jade to be free again, just as

Ammit has said. We'll get away together, move abroad. They'll never find us.' She glanced sidelong at the crocodile. 'Or Jade's body.'

Pushing up with his arms, Turner stood, toppling as his blurred senses kicked into life. Staggering across the floor, he gave the expectant reptile a wide birth, keeping well away from the slavering jaws straining on the chain.

He leant on the granite altar, wrapped a hand around the statue of Ammit and half closed his eyes as if in a trance. Out of sight of his captors, he pushed the cross from his pocket – the one that Molly Craggs had held so dear – into the body of one of the wax figures at the statue's feet. His plan was sketchy at best, but the only one that offered him a glimmer of hope.

After a long and silent pause, he inhaled deeply, opened his eyes and placed both hands on top of the shrine, palming the wax figure to keep it hidden. Slowly, he leant forward as if in prayer, moving the hand with the waxy bundle nearer the burning brazier on the top. As he turned to face Zoe, he dropped the wax figure into the brazier.

Fixing a distant stare on his now calm features, he said, 'You're right. Ammit has spoken to me. I know now what I must do. I must kill Jade myself to be free again.'

His voice appeared to have a new strength but in reality he was trying to drown out the noise of the wax melting and sizzling in the brazier. Tottering forwards, he lifted the sword cane from the floor and moved across the room to face his wife. Without a look back, he raised the blade to Jade's chest and pushed hard.

CHAPTER 24 – INTO THE DARKNESS

Zoe stood and wrapped her arms across her breast in a solo embrace, sobbing softly. All she'd ever wanted was to be loved and cared for, to be cherished and to find her soul mate. Now, with the help of the voice in her head from her revered demon, Nathen Turner had come back to her. Jade was dead and Turner could be free and stand at Zoe's side forever, just as Ammit had predicted. Inside, she felt cleansed of her sins. All she'd done was for this sole purpose – to be reborn into the life she'd once known with the man she loved. It wasn't her fault; for Zoe, the ends justified the means. It all made perfect sense.

At the other side of the room, Turner was working through a different set of emotions. One pushed up into his mind and surfaced above all the others. Hope. Joining in the madness was his only way of buying the time he needed, or thought he needed.

He could sense the room becoming colder as he silently called the name of Molly Craggs in his head. Jade's armpit was concealed by the black fabric; pushing the sword cane into the gap underneath would be enough to convince the siblings he'd killed his wife after being instructed by the demon figure of Ammit.

Jade was still slumped unconscious in the chair so he'd guessed they wouldn't know the difference. Of course, he had no real intention of harming his wife, and his mind spun as he tried to figure out his next move to get them both safely out of this mess. But now, even though he held a lethal weapon in his hand, the thought of using it against his captors made him feel sick. It just wasn't in his nature to deliberately lash out in anger and physically harm another; plus, he didn't have the skills for it. Knowing his luck, he'd end up stabbing himself.

Behind him, the wall candles in the alcove flickered and shot high flames in the air, burning the scenes of resurrection that sat behind them. The golden statue in the shrine tumbled hard onto the floor and shattered. Glittering shards of ceramic scattered across the room.

For the first time, Zoe looked uncertain. The sense of complete control and rush of power shrank inside her as her voice trembled. 'Nathen, what's happening? I feel cold, like an icy wind has blown in from somewhere. Hold me. Please hold me.'

Ignoring her, Turner spun to face the shrine. Above the brazier, a mist was forming, and through it the face of Molly Craggs gradually took shape – a cold dead face that now stared across at Zoe with hatred in its eyes. The furniture began to shake as though caught in an earthquake. Zoe screamed – a shriek that pierced Turner to the core.

Things were out of his control now. It was his deranged ex-girlfriend who'd given him the idea in the first place when she'd proudly told him about using the wax figures for her own rebirth; the same wax figures she'd said had the spells of resurrection inside them. The words he'd been unable to find poring through his ancient texts back home had helped him reach the spirit of Molly Craggs again. If his plan worked, this ethereal visitor would be enough to send his captors running for cover and give him enough time to escape with Jade and his friends. Turner looked on in wonder as Molly Craggs's pale dead body took shape and glided through the shrine towards Zoe.

Holding her hands in front of her face and screaming, Zoe ran blindly away from the spectre. 'Ammit, help me. Save me. I need you,' she shrieked.

As she sprinted across to gather up the fragments of the demon statue from the floor, she stumbled over one of the shards and fell forward on top of the chained crocodile.

Instinct took over, and the scaly reptile lashed its tail and bit hard. Conical teeth sank deeper as the crocodile swung Zoe's petite frame backwards and forwards, rolling over to manoeuvre her under its yellow-stained torso. Filled with bloodlust and the scent of the kill, the crocodile's huge claws ripped at her skin. Blood sprayed across the room. And then Zoe's shrieking stopped as the beast dragged her lifeless carcass back into the open panel in the alcove.

Williams and Turner stood rooted to the spot as the horror unfolded. This wasn't what Turner had had in mind when he'd summoned the spirit of Molly Craggs. He felt the bile rising in his stomach. All he'd wanted was to scare the siblings; he'd expected them to make a run for it. Once again, the feeling that he was the source of all this evil overwhelmed him and guilt made him shrink to the floor and cradle his knees, not knowing what he should do to help.

The ghostly figure of Molly Craggs watched, floating high above the carnal scene, and looked down as if fascinated. No, it was more than that – it was a look of satisfaction. Gliding back to the shrine, the vaporous figure bathed in the fire from the candles. Then the room was plunged into blackness.

With senses heightened by the dark, Turner could hear Williams panting somewhere off to his left. But he could also hear something else – the unmistakeable sound of padding paws moving down the corridor that led into the room. If Turner's hearing wasn't deceiving him, they'd shortly be joined by a bundle of seething fur that might be his escape from this hell.

Drugging the tea had been easy, but getting the right dose into the dog's bone had been a guess for Williams. He wasn't used to drugging anyone, let alone animals, so he'd ended up injecting the cocktail deep into the marrow of the dog's bone. And from the sounds of the approaching paws he'd pushed it too far inside to be effective for any length of time.

Outside, Kyle sniffed down the corridor into the darkness, hunting for his owner. Something was wrong, his doggy senses knew that – his master was in danger. The scent was stronger in this direction and he padded ahead, more cautiously now, the fur bristling on the back of his neck. Pricking up his ears, he stopped and listened. The sound of heavy breathing came from up ahead, along with a range of smells that he was unfamiliar with. Pressing his nose to the ground, his primal brain focused on hunting down his master. He crept forward and poked his head around the corner into the room. There was the sound of a man whimpering close to the door, but his scent was strange. This must be him, he thought, the one that had taken his master. Bounding ahead, he growled with all the ferocity he could muster and pounced into the darkness.

A wailing cry pierced the air, making Turner jump and scramble along the floor in the dark as Williams fought against the clawing bundle of fur tugging at his shirt. Williams scrabbled and kicked, then pushed desperately to his feet and ran backwards, trying to get his back against the wall, any wall. Bright light blinded his vision as the room lights flicked on. Seeing the exit, Williams ran for his life, frantically trying to escape the wrath of the growling hellhound.

He sprinted for the door and crumpled in a heap. There, standing with his police baton pushed forward and ready to strike, was Tony Coppenger tottering unstably on his feet. A huge bruise on the policeman's arm was already swelling from its impact with the locked lounge door after he'd stirred from his drugged sleep. Finding Kyle pacing restlessly, Lee comatose, and no sign of Turner, Tony's adrenalin-fuelled panic had smashed through the timber like balsa wood. He'd followed the dog as best he could in the darkness before finally finding the light switch.

The welt from the baton blow to Williams's forehead started to bleed as Tony jumped on top of him and punched him hard in the face. Seeing what looked like a dead Jade, slumped in the middle of the room and wearing a crazy black outfit, had enraged Tony, and he felt sure Williams was responsible. Tensing again for another punch, he stopped short as he glanced across to see Turner rocking backwards and forwards in the corner.

Amid the carnage, Turner mumbled incoherently to himself, unable to take it all in. Minutes ago, he'd been a man with no place to go, no form of escape except a flaky idea of pretending to join in Zoe's demonic delusions and scare his captors. Now they'd been dealt with in the most brutal way possible and he was free again. It had all happened so fast. His skin drained of all colour as his body went into shock.

Tony sprinted to catch him as Turner rolled heavily onto the floor.

'Nathen, can you hear me?' A voice called him back from the abyss. He wasn't sure he wanted to come but the voice was urgent, calling his name over and over again. Unwilling to open his eyes and face whatever new horror he'd see, he regained consciousness but played dead until he was sure it was safe. He felt responsible for everything that had happened, and the guilt lay like a millstone around his neck. His psychic life and his immoral past had caused all this. More lives ruined because of him. When would he ever be free of this legacy? All he'd ever wanted to do was to help people, but a sea of death and chaos seemed to engulf and drown him at every opportunity. And now it was taking his friends. Sandra Vaughan wouldn't be fighting for her life if it hadn't been for him. He'd also been an accessory to the murder of a client, Molly Craggs, and had unwittingly been a part of the brutal death of his deranged ex-girlfriend. This was all too much. He didn't want to wake up and face it all.

The voice called his name again, urging him back into the world. Slowly, he opened his eyes.

'Thank God,' a smiling face said above him. It was a beautiful face, with gentle green eyes that looked adoringly at him and swallowed him in their depths. Turner began to cry, tears flowing like a river down his face. Green Eyes held him close and spoke soft words of comfort into his ear. Police sirens blared from somewhere outside, but all Turner could sense was the warmth of the embrace – the tenderness of the touch that held him in a soothing blanket of love as he sobbed inconsolably against the face that snuggled next to his. He tried to move his arms but he'd been wrapped in something that crinkled and shimmered as he flexed. The voice urged him to keep still and reassured him he was safe now. Everything was going to be okay, it said.

Inside, Turner knew it would never be okay. Nobody could bring Molly Craggs or Zoe back to life. Maybe by using his psychic skill he'd be able to contact them again in the spirit world if he found the right words or the right ceremony. But talking to the spirits was like talking to a shadow of the people they'd once been. An empty shell where once a living, breathing person had existed – someone who could touch, and taste, and laugh. And love. He of all people knew that.

The voice called his name again and he looked back into those eyes. The beautiful green eyes that seemed to see inside him and stare at his soul.

'How do you feel?' the voice said, and he could sense the soft breath on his cheek.

Through bleary eyes he focused on the face next to his

and remembered. Yes, he remembered. He saw again in his mind's eye how he'd lifted the sword cane and thrust it through Jade's chest. The black lace fabric had made it easy to see the gap under her arm and he'd plunged it through, pretending to struggle as the blade eased into the opening concealed by the dress. Jade, my beautiful Jade, he thought as she kissed him and stroked his hair.

'I thought we'd lost you. You were so pale,' Jade said.

After being revived by the paramedics, Jade had refused any further medical treatment until she'd spoken to her husband and made sure he was all right. Certainly he was alive, but there was a sadness and pain behind his eyes that broke her heart.

Turner wanted to speak, tried to speak, but the words wouldn't come. All he managed was 'I love you.'

Across from the lovers, Lee Melone woke from a deep slumber on the couch. Exhausted from the past few days, and having drunk more than his fair share of tea, he'd had a beautiful and dreamless sleep, his first unbroken rest in days. As he stretched lazily and yawned, he saw Turner in a chair opposite the settee, wrapped in a silver survival blanket, Jade next to him, stroking his hair. The dog lay curled over Turner's toes, keeping a watchful eye on the proceedings.

'What did I miss?' he said.

.

CHAPTER 25 – TRUTH AND LIES

Leaning back in his chair, with his left arm hooked over the back, Williams sat opposite the uniformed officer and asked for the fourth time whether he could smoke. After the predicted refusal, he harrumphed, turned to his lawyer and mumbled 'Police brutality' under his breath. Mr No-Claim-No-Fee legal scumbag nodded vigorously in agreement and was about to launch into a speech about human rights when the door opened.

Detective Inspector Ruby Robinson rolled across the room, pulled out a chair and collapsed into it. The stress of the job made her eat, and carrying around the subsequent weight made her tired and filled with self-loathing. She covered her dissatisfaction with herself by pretending as best she could to like everybody else.

Smiling across at Williams, she said, 'Thank you for your statement, Mr Williams. I just need to go over one or two things.'

Flicking open the manila folder on the table, she skipped over the personal-details section and began to read through Williams's statement, written in tidy black pen by the uniformed officer:

Mr Williams was entertaining guests at his home when he began to feel unwell. After drinking some tea that his sister, Zoe, had made, he believes he lapsed into unconsciousness. When he awoke he heard shouting and ran to investigate. As he left the lounge (where he was entertaining his visitors) he noted that his guests also seemed to be unconscious. After tracing the sounds of the raised voices, he entered a room at the back of the house that used to be the old library. In the room, he found a Mr Nathen Turner (address details below) brandishing what looked like a sword. Mr Williams states that Mr Turner was threatening his sister with the sword and that she was in a state of terror. Across the room, Mr Turner's wife, Jade Turner, had been bound to a chair and Mr Williams believes that Mr Turner had brought his wife to the vicarage property in an attempt to kill her and frame Mr Williams for the crime. Mr Williams believes that his sister had interrupted the proceedings when she'd brought her pet reptile indoors to feed it, and Mr Turner was attempting to silence her. As Mr Williams watched, he saw Mr Turner approach his sister with the blade and then start pulling viciously at her hair, trying to release the head covering that she used to hide her facial disability. Mr Turner's inability to release the head covering appeared to enrage him further and he deliberately pushed Mr Williams's sister head first towards the pet reptile (a large Nile crocodile). Acting in self-defence, the reptile had instinctively reacted and fatally wounded his sister. Fleeing for his life, Mr Williams was brutally attacked at the doorway by one of his other visitors – a Detective Inspector Tony Coppenger – and rendered unconscious ...

Williams patted at the welt on his crown from the baton strike. The gesture caused DI Robinson to look up and she scanned his every move like a sniffer dog on a scent.

Robinson cleared her throat. 'If I read this correctly, you believe your sister put something in the tea that rendered yourself and your visitors unconscious. Is that what you're stating – for the record?' She glanced across at the whirring tape recorder on the table as if to emphasise the point.

Wincing and stroking at his head injury, Williams said, 'Yes. My sister often put chloral hydrate in her tea to help her sleep. With her facial disability it was difficult for her to rest. I must've picked up the wrong teapot. She has a prescription for it. You can ask her.'

Then he began to sob as if just realising he'd spoken about his sister as if she'd survived the horrible events. Having thought long and hard about his approach to clear his name, Williams had created a version of events to blame Turner and put his sister and himself in the clear. Family loyalty came before friendship in his eyes, and the last thing he was prepared to do was have his sister's name dragged through the dirt. Of course, he knew his story was farfetched, but it would be his word against Turner's and his rather dubious assortment of acquaintances. All he needed to do was create some reasonable doubt in the minds of the police, and he hoped his skills as an accomplished liar would see him through.

Unmoved by Williams's onset of emotion, the detective continued. 'And you say that Mr Turner was clearly threatening your sister when you found them together in the room – the old library? And you have no knowledge of how

Mr Turner got into the house, or even, and rather bizarrely, how he was able to sneak in and bind his wife to a chair with the intent to kill her at your property?'

Williams's sobbing intensified and the scumbag lawyer passed over a handkerchief and patted him reassuringly on the arm. 'Mr Turner screamed obscenities at my sister and made fun of her – you know, rude comments about her looks. It was like watching a crazy man. They used to have a relationship and my sister dumped him. I don't think he ever got over it. How can anyone be so heartless as to mock a disabled person? I think Mr Turner was trying to frame me for his wife's murder after we had harsh words following my clairvoyant show; he wanted revenge. He's never liked me and personally I think he's unstable. I can only assume he entered through the back door – we never lock it. It's common knowledge that Mr Turner and his wife have been having marital problems and I believe he wanted rid of her for good.'

Hoping that throwing in the disability line about his sister would garner some sympathy, Williams chanced a look across the table to see if he'd got any reaction from the detective. He hadn't.

DI Robinson leant forward on her elbows to get a closer look at her detainee. Pointing down at a colour image of the sword cane found in Williams's house, she said, 'And this sword cane – the one you allege Mr Turner used – is it yours?'

Realising his sobbing approach wasn't working, Williams put down the handkerchief and made eye contact with the detective. 'No, it is not. I've never seen it before. Mr Turner must have brought it with him, meaning to use it to kill his wife.' His stare remained fixed, unblinking as he spoke.

'I see,' DI Robinson said, returning the stare. She'd played this game enough times and, although Williams didn't know it yet, he was opposite a woman who could sniff out a lie at fifty paces. Long experience had taught her to be patient, to allow the witness time to dig themselves a big enough hole, one that she'd delight in burying them in. 'And this pet reptile – a Nile crocodile, I believe. You have a licence for it, I assume?'

Williams nodded and mumbled a yes, knowing full well that he didn't. They'd smuggled it out from a carnival show down south when it was only a youngster about two feet long. At the time, he'd believed that if his sister had something to care for, something dependent on her, it might improve her state of mind. She'd insisted on the crocodile; her fascination with her imagined demon had seen to that. If he'd known back then it would grow into the giant it was now, he'd never have let it happen. The thing terrified him, and Zoe would often threaten him with it if he tried to stop her doing what she wanted.

Shuffling through the papers in front of her, DI Robinson said, 'Well, in that case, I'm sure we'll find the relevant licence papers at your house, won't we? You also state that DI Coppenger attacked you without warning in the doorway. Again please, for the record, is that correct?'

Williams folded his arms and sat back indignantly. 'Yes, it is, and I want to make a formal complaint.'

DI Robinson reached down into a briefcase on the floor and removed a folder with a case-file number and 'Laboratory reports' emblazoned across the front.

'For the tape I will now read out some of the early forensic findings from Mr Williams's house.' Pulling herself upright, she smiled. 'Mr Williams, the lab reports of the china cups from your living room show no evidence that you drank from them. The blood and urine samples, which you freely submitted, have no trace of chloral hydrate. A syringe with your fingerprints on, discovered by scene-of-crime officers in your kitchen, contains a strong solution of chloral hydrate identical to the contents of the Welldorm Elixir your sister had been given on prescription. In short, there's *no* evidence to suggest that *you* were drugged, but there is evidence to suggest that *you* were actually the one who dosed the tea with the syringe. Also, there are no traces of Mr Turner's fingerprints on the manacles that were used to secure his wife to the chair, but there are multiple clear prints from both you and your sister. So it would appear that it was, in fact, you and your sister who secured Mr Turner's wife to the chair.'

Across the table, the scumbag lawyer appeared to be realising that this was heading into his no-fee category, and he looked at the floor.

DI Robinson pressed on, beginning to enjoy herself. 'Furthermore, there's no forensic evidence that indicates Mr Turner handled the facial covering – the silicone mask – your sister used to hide her disfigurement. Had he violently tugged at her hair as you say, then we would expect to find some trace of that. But there are grounds to suggest that both you and your sister *did* handle the Egyptian mask.'

She'd saved the best bit until last and lifted a clear evidence bag from the back of the file containing a till receipt from an antique shop.

'Finally, this receipt, found at your property, shows that you purchased an antique sword cane from a shop in London just over a year ago. We've matched the dealer's record with the sword cane found at the scene, and it's the same one. So, not only had you seen the weapon before, but it was *you* who purchased it.'

Flicking the folder closed, the detective leant back and smiled. 'More forensic results from the DNA testing will come in over the next week or so. Oh, and we also found a significant quantity of dog hair in the room where the alleged attack by Mr Turner took place, and on your shirt, but your statement doesn't appear to mention the presence of any canine. Have you anything to say, Mr Williams?'

Williams looked at the scumbag lawyer, then back at the detective.

'No comment.'

Over in the investigation hub, Tony Coppenger was getting what was commonly called the hairdryer treatment from his chief inspector.

'Whacking some bugger in the head with a baton when you're off-duty and punching him in the face is not bloody reasonable force.' The chief took a step closer so their noses were almost touching. 'How the hell am I supposed to justify this to the IPCC?'

Glowing like an over-ripe tomato, the chief poked Tony hard in the chest to make sure he'd got the point. 'You're on leave, effective immediately. Now bugger off.'

As he was pushed out the door of the glass-lined office,

Tony was met with a wave of catcalls and 'you got off lightly there, son' jibes from his fellow officers.

Since the discovery that Molly Craggs's death and Sandra Vaughan's attack were by the same hand, coordination of the investigation had been moved to the Scarborough Investigation Hub to ease the administrative burden of evidence collection from the local force. On the incident board pushed against the far wall, someone had written *Did they see it coming? The psychic killing*, across the top, using the typical dark humour that surrounded such investigations. Underneath, various gory scene-of-crime images and scribbled notes highlighted the key parts of the case.

Embarrassed and needing to flee the banter of his colleagues, Tony headed out of the room as if a tiger were on his tail.

Downstairs in a holding cell, Turner contemplated life, the universe and whether he really wanted to use the steel toilet bolted to the wall. He'd provided a detailed statement hours ago and had been left to stew in this white-walled cage ever since.

After leaving Jade for screening tests at the local hospital, he felt isolated and alone. Lee had come and gone according to the amiable guard who made the odd appearance outside the viewing hatch in the door. Apparently, 'I slept through the whole thing' didn't take long to write down and Lee was impatient to call the hospital and check on Sandra.

Turner had been amazed at how his housemate now seemed to be coping with the attack on his girlfriend after surviving his suicidal night, freezing on the pier, and the events at the vicarage. It was like he'd come to terms with it after his own near-death experience and the horror at Williams's house – albeit he'd slept through it – and decided that his life was, after all, worth living. Now his focus appeared to be on making sure Sandra could be nursed back to health rather than his own feelings. Lee was positive, upbeat even, about the future and Turner hoped he was right.

The isolation in the cell drew Turner back into his own guilt. This entire veil of death had been pulled down because of him and what he did for a living, or rather had once done. The spectre of his past simply wouldn't leave him alone.

Zoe and he had met at one of his psychic gigs where he'd pretended to contact a host of spirits for an adoring crowd. At the time, it had made him feel good, bringing messages of comfort and closure to as many strangers as he could. Some of those strangers were now loyal friends. The fact that he made it all up on the spot hadn't bothered him back then. But when a real spirit called, a genuine lost soul needing help, he'd known he had to quit. Sustaining the lie was too much for him to bear. Changing the business into psychic coaching had worked well. His drive to help others could be satisfied and he got to meet some fascinating people with real ability. That's all he'd ever wanted to do – help others.

Then a knock on his front door had changed his life. Molly Craggs had needed his help and now she was dead. And it was his fault. Inside, he knew he should never have accepted her request; the whole thing had felt wrong to him at the time but he hadn't had the strength to turn her away. What was he, some white knight ever rescuing damsels in distress? Well, this damsel never returned from his quest and her journey had ended in the most brutal way possible.

Before he could continue his morbid internal discussion, there was a rattle of keys and the cell door opened.

Seeing the familiar dumpy figure of DI Robinson entering the room was like somebody had thrown Turner a lifeline in the sea of despondency that was drowning him. They'd met before on another case years ago and she'd helped him above and beyond the call of duty. She still looked like her clothes were fighting for dear life to hang on to her swelling frame.

Smiling, she walked in heavily and shook his hand. Although there was tiredness in her eyes, Turner could sense an air of satisfaction in the way she held herself.

In truth, Robinson held a bit of a candle for Nathen Turner. There was a lot to admire about the man, and some of her friends who'd met him socially spoke in glowing terms about this gentle giant. In her work, she'd hauled in many so-called psychics who'd swindled money off gullible clients or miraculously found themselves included in a lucrative will. But Turner wasn't like that, at least not in her experience. There was an air about him, something otherworldly behind his eyes that suggested he'd seen and experienced things not meant for this mortal plane.

Pushing over a piece of paper secured to a clipboard, she asked him politely to sign and said, 'That's it, Nathen. You're free to go. We've got a smartly dressed clairvoyant canary singing away upstairs who's put you in the clear.'

Turner knew at once she meant Williams. How she'd managed to get behind the clairvoyant's ability to manipulate and lie his way out of it, Turner had no idea, and thought it was best that way.

In reality, it had proved easier than she'd thought. Faced with the forensic findings that showed clearly Williams had been lying, his no-win, no-fee legal expert had suggested that truth was the only option if Williams didn't want to face the rest of his life in prison.

Sourced from a pool of lawyers, with little experience outside of accident claims against guilt-ridden employers, a murder enquiry was not this particular legal vulture's forte.

Turner signed and shook his head. 'Are you sure? I mean ... I'm free to go?'

Robinson nodded. 'You'll be needed at the trial, and make sure we can contact you if you're travelling away from the area. But, yes, it looks like it's over.'

Without thinking, Turner stood up and embraced the detective, tears flowing down his cheeks.

CHAPTER 26 – AWAY FROM IT ALL

Turner had been to two different funerals in as many days and his mood had hit rock bottom. After two tearful affairs for Molly and Zoe, he sat in the corner of Sandra Vaughan's welcome-home party, watching Lee down as much alcohol as his body could handle. Lee had hired the main room at the Jolly Roger pub where Sandra worked part time. For some reason that had escaped Turner, he'd also booked a karaoke machine, and two barmaids were currently belting out 'Mamma Mia' in a style that had alley cats running for cover.

In the corner, an argument had broken out about a botched drinks order. Apparently one of the guys had asked for a snakebite – the fifty-fifty lager/cider drink – and his friend had misheard and brought him a steak pie instead. The whole scene looked like a typical Friday night out rather than a respectful celebration of a life brought back from the brink.

Looking at Sandra cradled in a wheelchair next to Lee, Turner was in no mood for celebration. Yes, she was alive, but the full aftermath of her ordeal remained unknown. If she'd ever walk again was still in the hands of a higher power.

But both Lee and Sandra seemed focused on the present and not his pessimistic view of the future. They laughed happily together, enjoying the evening.

Looking for respite away from the noise, Turner headed outside into the cool afternoon air and gazed across the harbour. Fishing boats chugged their way back in, crammed full with tottering lobster and crab pots that dripped wetly onto the deck. Seeing the men haul their catch onto the quay brought back memories of his father, who'd spent a lifetime at sea doing exactly the same thing. It was a simpler life, he thought, than his chosen profession, and one that had never led to the murder and carnage that surrounded Turner.

One of the fishermen spotted him and shouted a greeting that was lost in the cacophony of the boat engine. Automatically, he waved back and watched the boat motor into the harbour. All his life his father had taken pride in the brotherhood of the sea, where danger brought men together to join forces against all that nature could throw at them. Many fishermen had kept in touch with Turner after his father's passing, and he'd wile away hours over a pint, swapping tall tales of his dad's exploits just to keep his memories alive.

The word from the police was that Williams was likely to face an automatic life sentence for conspiracy and incitement to murder, as he'd clearly had some agreement with his sister about the brutal death of Molly Craggs, even though he personally had not done the deed himself. Whether life actually meant life in this age of human rights and civil liberties, Turner very much doubted, plus Williams was a clever and cunning man. If there was a way to reduce his custodial sentence, he felt sure Williams would find it. What if, in ten or twenty years' time, he bumped into Williams as a free man? Or maybe Williams would hunt him down when he got out and seek retribution for Turner's part in all this.

Maybe he should get away, move to a different country and re-invent himself. But Turner had no qualifications or other skills to speak of, and no hobbies he could turn into moneymaking opportunities. All he'd ever done was immerse himself into a spiritual life – that was his only hobby and his chosen profession.

A hand tapped him on the back and he looked around to see Tony's smiling face. 'You okay? I'm worried about you.'

Forcing a smile, Turner said, 'I'm fine,' when he really meant, 'No I'm a wreck and I don't know what to do about it.'

'Yeah, right, and I'm the Queen of Sheba. You're not fine and you bloody know it.' Tony moved around to stand in front of the psychic and put his arm on his shoulder. It was a gesture that meant to say 'I'm here for you' but it looked more like he was arresting him.

'Have you heard that scene-of-crime have found the campervan Zoe used to travel around in?'

Tuner shook his head.

'It was parked up in one of the garages at the back of the vicarage along with an old hatchback.'

Turner stayed quiet, waiting for the next revelation that would blow his world apart.

Taking in a deep breath as if he were building up to something, Tony said, 'There were a load of files in the campervan – some with newspaper clippings from marriages, births and deaths columns, that kind of thing. Most of the other files held personal information on people who attended the clairvoyant shows and detailed what they were into. I guess they used the material to dupe the punters during the performance.'

At least that explained how Zoe, in her Egyptian guise, had been so accurate in her readings, Turner thought. She'd gathered all the information pre-show. All it needed was a convincing psychic-style act to deliver the knowledge she'd accumulated, and she'd certainly had that.

Tony swallowed hard and stuttered. 'And ... Z-Zoe had written a diary.'

'What do you mean, a diary? You telling me she wrote it all down?'

Backing up half a step, Tony glanced around uneasily, not sure how much he should tell his friend. What the hell, he thought. He was on compulsory leave. What could they do to him for leaking the information? He looked past Turner, not wanting to make eye contact. 'Apparently, she'd set herself deliberately on fire, trying to kill herself after your relationship ended. It wasn't an accident. Her neighbour saved her life, so Zoe tried again and cut her face. In the diary, she says she tried to cut her throat, but she'd drunk too much alcohol and downed a few pills. It was Williams who found her that time, and he rushed her to the hospital. After the second attempt, Williams bought the vicarage and made her live with him so he could keep an eye on her. They've lived there for a while, not the few months he told us.'

Lost for words, Turner looked out to sea, trying not to think about what his ex-girlfriend had been through. Or about what he felt he'd *made* her do.

Feeling committed to tell the rest of the tale, Tony continued. 'In the diary, she says she had no purpose, no reason to live anymore, and she knew she couldn't go out easily in public with her facial disfigurement. So, after a few tries with modified paint-spray masks and the like to hide the worst, her brother found this guy who could make lifelike masks. There were loads of different outfits in the campervan. A few veiled black dresses, wigs, walking clothes, and spray masks with weird faces painted on the outside. It's like she was trying on, and acting out, different personas rather than be who she was. The problem was that she ended up looking like an Egyptian. I don't know how this happened; it's not clear in the diary.'

Turner knew how it had happened – Williams had told him. He stayed quiet and urged Tony to carry on.

Seeing the pain etched on Turner's face, the policeman thought he might've gone too far passing on the information. Reluctantly, he continued, looking at the sagging figure with pity in his eyes. 'Anyway, the ever-resourceful Hugh Williams decided to use the new Egyptian look to his advantage and created a part for her in his show. They've toured all over; a lot of the time with carnival and sideshow-type acts. The diary is pretty upbeat after that. It's as if she'd found a new lease of life and a way to move on from her past. Then the writing in the diary mentions someone called Ammit, who talked to her and advised her what to do. We're still trying to track this Ammit character down and see what he has to say.'

Good luck tracking Ammit down, Turner thought, images of the demon statue flashing through his head. You're about three thousand years too late.

Tony moved to head back inside, thinking he'd said enough already, but Turner pulled him back by the coat. 'There's more, isn't there? Please. I need to know.'

Looking at the psychic, the policeman felt sorry for him. It was like someone had sucked the air out of Turner as he hunched over, pleading for the information.

Rubbing his hand roughly over his smooth chin, Tony said, 'Okay, I'll tell you, but keep it to yourself.' He rocked backwards and forwards on his feet and took a decided interest in the floor. 'Then you turned up at the clairvoyant show with Jade on your arm, and the diary talks about Zoe asking this guy Ammit for advice. It doesn't make a lot of sense to be honest. There's a real fury in the writing and the pages are wrinkled as though they've got wet at some point. Reading it is like following a madman's journey into a very dark place.'

Turner looked out to sea, thinking things over. His heart raced. It was all too horrible and crazy to take in. How could such insanity have enveloped his old girlfriend? Her tears had probably flooded the pages as she wrote about the man who'd torn her heart out and then paraded his wife in front of her. His mind flooded with images of Zoe's smiling face, heading merrily from bar to bar in Whitby's cramped streets, years ago. The love he'd felt for her bubbled inside, but gave him no comfort. Sure, back when he'd known her, Zoe had shown signs of mania and possessiveness, but nothing that could've escalated to this. Yes, she was quirky, weird even, but so was he, and it had bound them together for a while.

Questions tumbled through his brain. What if all human

beings had mental-health issues locked away inside and simply didn't know it? he wondered, now questioning what it would take to tip him into madness. Hidden, base animal instincts hung over from primordial times, now forced to conform to an artificial existence full of concrete towers, aeroplanes and computer technology. Maybe so-called civilised humans had learnt to keep their savage, uncultured demons concealed, locked away in silence, deep in their soul, in a drive for social acceptance in modern society. The silent demon hidden in the soul of Zoe, which had called out to her through a prescription-drug-fuelled haze, had insisted on being heard before unleashing chaos. What would it take for Turner to unleash his demons and make him harm and even kill others? Hate, intolerance, revenge, greed, or even love? He doubted he was capable of such brutality, but history was littered with tales of atrocities carried out in the name of these emotions.

It looked to Turner like Lee was now drowning his demons in alcohol as his way of coping with Sandra's near-death experience and uncertain future. But those demons would still be there when Lee sobered up, clawing at him, screaming into his nightmares.

Not trusting himself to speak, Turner's eyes wandered over to the beach. He watched a couple of tourists walking hand in hand along the surf line. Normal life unfolded before him while his own proved to be anything but.

Growing uncomfortable with the silence and Turner's clouded gaze, Tony grabbed him by the arm. 'Nathen, are you sure you're okay?'

No response.

Turner's gaze had moved over to the amusement arcades as a group of teens sat munching fish and chips outside. Eating with one hand, they held their smartphones with the other, obsessed with the idea that they'd missed the latest titbit of useless information.

Tony grabbed both arms, pulled Turner around to face him and looked at the pale, drawn features. He'd never seen him like this before – it looked like a part of Turner had died inside and poisoned him from within.

As if moving in slow motion, Turner lifted his head and said, 'This is all my fault. All of it. When I turned up at the clairvoyant show with Jade it triggered all this mayhem.'

Hesitantly, Tony nodded. He knew this was the case – like he'd told Turner, it was all in the diary.

Pulling away again, Turner returned to his inner world. Leaving his ex-girlfriend had moved her to suicide and drug-induced delusion, he thought, his self-worth plunging to a new low. Then, to rub salt in the wound, he'd shown up at one of her shows with his beautiful wife on his arm. The hurt Zoe must have felt – no wonder she'd locked herself away in the campervan after the show. She must've been crying her eyes out, every tear filling a cup of insanity that was already overflowing.

Turner had seen her silhouetted figure in the campervan talking to a statue. That must have been the golden figure of the demon, Ammit, which she held so dear, its imagined voice filling her mind with crazy ideas of retribution. And in defence of Williams, maybe having his sister focused on maniacal vengeance was preferable to another suicide attempt. The man Turner had known would never have contemplated colluding in such a thing, but perhaps Williams had become trapped as soon as Zoe had acted on her fantasy and killed Molly Craggs. Williams was certainly going to pay for his part in it now. They all were in different ways.

Turner thanked Tony for trusting him with the information and pushed back into the squalling wall of sound in the bar. The arguing guys in the corner were now drowning their squabble in pints of snakebite and tucking into a steak pie each, laughing and pointing at each other. The two barmaids on the karaoke had moved from singing Abba melodies to belting out 'YMCA' at the top of their lungs while encouraging the crowd to join in with the movements of the song.

Jade spotted Tony walking back in behind her husband and intercepted him to find out what they'd been talking about. Nodding and seeming to come to a decision, she talked urgently with the policeman and headed to the quieter back room to make a phone call.

As if he carried a heavy weight on his back, Turner flopped at a side table and watched Jade weave her way back through the crowd.

Shouting above the noise, she said, 'Right it's all fixed. I'm taking you away for a break from all this. Tony will sort it out with the police and make sure they know where we are. He said he'll stay at our place so he can keep an eye on Lee and Sandra, and also help with the dog.' She kissed Turner on the cheek. 'You need a change of scenery and I've got just the thing.'

Watching Turner slump into depression broke her heart, but never one to shy away from a problem, she was facing it head on. A new environment and old memories was what he needed – memories of happier times to replace the morose ones in his head. After telephoning her airline colleagues and pulling in a few favours, she'd swiftly arranged what, in her eyes, was the perfect tonic.

She pushed a drink into his hand and said, 'Drink up, my love. You've got to pack.'

A little over thirty-six hours later they were sitting in a bar at the top end of the Las Vegas strip. The place didn't so much have a redneck vibe – more like it had been immersed up to its denim dungarees in hillbilly moonshine and then painted with the Confederate flag. On the other side of the room, a full-figured woman sat astride a bucking bronco that did its mechanical best to throw her off onto the rubber mats. Sweaty men leant against the fake wooden fence surround, eagerly admiring her plump behind as it bounced and gyrated on the wide saddle. To their right, a huge muddy pit lay in front of a short stage and a guy on the PA announced the arrival of the next pair of mud wrestlers to a series of yee-haws from the crowd. Two bikini-clad beauties glared at each other before the bigger one unceremoniously dumped the other into the slippery pit.

Jade beamed at Turner, who laughed uproariously as the muddy girls tried to get a grip on each other and fell face first into the ooze.

'This is great, isn't it?' she said.

Still laughing at the slip-sliding antics of the bikini babes, Turner didn't hear her over the screams of the crowd.

She tried again, louder this time. 'I said, this is great, isn't it?'

'Yes,' he said, pointing at the steel bucket on the floor, 'and it's the first time I've had to order beer in a bucket.'

The house special – bottles of cold lager in ice that filled a bucket to the brim.

They were already on their second and he watched as smiling tourists grabbed a refill from the bar and sat down. It looked like a rowdy group of farmers returning from the milking shed of an alcoholic cow who also happened to run a brewery.

Turner took a large pull on his drink and snorted it out as Bikini Babe One slipped and fell face first again. The shadow of the past that had been haunting him was gradually drifting away like an old and partially forgotten nightmare. Being back in Las Vegas thrilled him – he simply loved the place. The glitz and glamour coupled with a sense of just-out-of-reach danger drew him in and flooded his thoughts. He'd first met Jade on a flight back from Vegas, and since then had always thought of it as a lucky place.

After more laughter, and faced with an empty beer bucket, they headed out into the dry air on the sidewalk. The wave of heat after the cool air conditioning made them swoon and fall into each other's arms, giggling. Swaying, they made their way down the strip, stopping at the bursting fountains of the Bellagio; columns of water rocketed into the air accompanied by an upbeat soundtrack that made them sway in time. A crowd was already pushed up against the fence, watching the display. Jade pulled Turner to one side and kissed him.

Looking into her beautiful green eyes, he'd never felt more in love. She seemed part of him and somehow understood him at a primal level. Getting away was exactly what he'd needed; he just hadn't known it up until now.

He kissed her lightly on the forehead. 'You know, Jade, the more I think about it, I feel sure it really was the spirit of your mother that came through to Princess Amunet on stage that night to warn you. We know the princess act was a con by the two siblings, and I know her falling over at the end can't have been part of it. Your mother's spirit's still here, protecting you.'

'I know,' she said, and kissed him again.

Turner raised an eyebrow but let the comment lie. Maybe he wasn't the only one blessed with spiritual insight after all.

The fountains sprayed to a halt, accompanied by cheers from the crowd, so they kept walking down the packed street, weaving between the colourful tourists that littered the pavement. Turner had no idea what he would do when he got home – carry on along his spiritual path or try to change to something new if he couldn't face it after the trauma of the past few weeks. These were thoughts for another day. Right now, he was happy and in the company of the one person he truly adored.

They pulled up short as they walked in front of the glowing face of the Luxor. Behind the overhead monorail, a large illuminated sphinx sat sentry-like in front of a huge obsidian pyramid that beamed a bright xenon light into the evening sky from its summit. Tottering palm trees swayed behind a giant stone obelisk covered in hieroglyphics, the word 'Luxor' written vertically down the side. It was as if a Disneyland version of ancient Egypt had come to Vegas and sat amid the rushing traffic and pulsing nightlife.

Turner tugged at Jade's sleeve to urge her to walk past. 'I've seen enough relics of ancient Egypt for one lifetime; let's keep going.'

She giggled and yanked him forward. 'C'mon, Nathen, face your fear. Let's go inside. The worst thing that can happen is we'll gamble away some money. At least we'll have fun losing it.'

Lagging behind, Turner looked across the street to a gigantic billboard advertising one of the Luxor's resident shows for a cool-looking magician called Criss Angel. It was the name of the magic show that caught his attention. One single word was emblazoned across the bottom.

Believe.

The word tumbled through Turner's mind. His current world was a product of what he'd lived. He needed to believe he could create a new future – to re-invent himself in a way that left the horror of his past far behind. And, above all else, he needed to believe that he could make it happen. Gradually, his life was teaching him how to live it, if only he could stay alive long enough to learn the lesson.

Jade's voice broke through his thoughts. 'Tell me, Nathen,' she said, pulling playfully at his shirt, 'have you got any other ex-girlfriends I should know about?'

'Yeah, loads,' he said, kissing her on the cheek.

Smiling broadly, Nathen Turner walked past the glowing sphinx without a second look and stepped inside.

DISCOVER MORE ABOUT THE NATHEN TURNER THRILLERS:

Want to read more about the background to the Nathen Turner stories and explore the haunting settings? Sign up for the *Haunting Tales* newsletter at **www.andrewlangley.co.uk** and join the growing group of Nathen Turner fans.

Andrew also posts regular updates and special offers on Twitter. Connect with him at **@mirroronthesoul** to keep right up to date with the latest news.

If you liked this book, please tell others about it! Andrew really appreciates all the positive reviews from readers on Amazon, Barnes & Noble, Goodreads etc. Thank you for your support; it's very much appreciated.

Nathen Turner also features in *Mirror on the Soul* and *Dark Nights of the Soul*, available from your favourite bookstore.

ALSO AVAILABLE:

The first Nathen Turner novel:

Mirror on the Soul

ISBN 978-0-9554137-1-1

Meet Nathen Turner, successful psychic medium, who doesn't believe in ghosts or the supernatural. He's an ordinary man with an extraordinary gift – he just doesn't know it yet.

Using observation, guesswork and the occasional conjuring trick, Nathen Turner pretends he can communicate with the spirit world and predict the future. From Las Vegas to his hometown of Whitby, he is paid well for his 'special abilities'. But it is all an act – Turner doesn't believe in ghosts, spirits or any form of afterlife. Then, during a sham psychic performance, the ghostly voice of a young girl calls out to him. Someone, or something, is trying to make contact. Turner the deceiver is becoming Turner the believer, and he can't shake the feeling that he's being watched. Unwittingly, the self-professed 'fake' psychic medium has opened a very real door into the supernatural. Now the dead are talking back and the only thing on their mind is revenge …

'GRIPPING AND ORIGINAL, WITH UNFORGETTABLE CHARACTERS.'

Jack Magnus for US review site, Readers' Favorite.

Awarded a 5-star review.

Dark Nights of the Soul

ISBN 978-0-9554137-5-9

Wilderness, witchcraft and a Scottish wildcat. The Scottish Highlands hold a deadly secret for maverick psychic Nathen Turner in this second novel from the fast-paced supernatural thriller series.

When the onset of multiple sclerosis blinds photographer Mike Fletcher, his world is torn apart. Losing everything he holds dear, he heads to the remote Scottish Highlands to re-assess his life. On Fletcher's first night, a freak lightning storm unearths a bizarre symbol in the building next to his croft. The symbol appears to be painted in blood, and the blood is still wet. After a local fisherman tells him the property is on a site renowned for ancient witchcraft, Fletcher becomes uneasy, thinking his self-imposed isolation was not such a great idea. Is this just a childish prank or something far more deadly? Turner must unravel the mystery before it is too late.

'THIS BOOK GRABBED ME BY THE THROAT FROM THE VERY FIRST PAGE. WOW! I LOVED IT.'

Tracy A. Fischer for US review site, Readers' Favorite. Awarded a 5-star review.

www.ingramcontent.com/pod-product-compliance
Lightning Source LLC
Chambersburg PA
CBHW021421110726
47901CB00008B/2246